SCONE COLD DEAD

A GRAY WHALE INN MYSTERY

KAREN MACINERNEY

GRAY WHALE PRESS

Other books in the Gray Whale Inn Mysteries:

The Gray Whale Inn Mysteries

Murder on the Rocks

Dead and Berried

Murder Most Maine

Berried to the Hilt

Brush With Death

Death Runs Adrift

Whale of a Crime

Claws for Alarm

Cookbook: The Gray Whale Inn Kitchen

Blueberry Blues (A Gray Whale Inn Short Story)

Pumpkin Pied (A Gray Whale Inn Short Story)

Iced Inn (A Gray Whale Inn Short Story)

I'm good at a lot of things. Whipping up sour cream coffee cake before I've finished my first cup of coffee. Being polite to guests who complain that there's no room service at 2 a.m. Cutting up pineapples without removing the tips of my fingers.

I am not, unfortunately, good at watercolor.

It was the first day of my niece Gwen's inaugural art class at Cranberry Island's brand-new Art Guild. With the help of some big donors—and local developer Murray Selfridge—Gwen, my husband John, and a few other artists had worked together to turn Fernand LaChaise's property into an art school and gallery again. I, along with several other islanders, had eagerly signed up for classes—not just because I wanted to support Gwen, but because I'd always wanted to try my hand at painting.

So far, it wasn't going well.

"Is that supposed to be water?" my classmate Charlene asked, pointing a paintbrush at my page. She was dressed nattily, as usual, in hip-hugger jeans that clung to her ample, curvy figure and a gorgeous, green cashmere sweater that contrasted beautifully with her caramel-streaked hair. Charlene was the island's postmistress and the proprietor of Cranberry Island's only store; she was also my best friend.

"Yeah," I said.

"Same here," she said, pointing to her page. Although she was a wizard with a makeup brush, she, too, seemed to be struggling with the whole painting thing.

"What am I doing wrong?" I asked as I stared at the large, blotchy blue spot on my formerly pristine piece of white paper.

Gwen drifted over and examined my attempt at watercolor. "There's a lot of pigment on there," she said, a line appearing between her delicate brows. She looked gorgeous and artistic as always, in a flowing skirt and a crinkly red-velvet blouse that accented her dark hair and ivory skin. Marriage seemed to suit her; since she and local lobsterman Adam Thrackton had tied the knot just before Christmas, she'd seemed happier than ever. Her outfit reflected her artistic abilities, as did the detailed, evocative watercolor paintings that graced the walls of the gallery next door. I, on the other hand, was more pragmatically clad—as usual—in jeans and a plaid shirt that I wore untucked to hide the evidence of a few-too-many blueberry muffins. And my painting? Well...

"Did you do a wash with water first?" my talented niece asked, trying to diagnose the problem.

"You mean, coat the page with water? Yes, I did. And then I just dabbed on some paint from there."

"Ah. That could be the issue. You might want to make a little pool of water on the palette and dab a little bit of pigment in it instead of taking it straight from the tray," she suggested. "What makes watercolor special is its transparency."

"Okay. I'll try that," I said, and moved to crumple up the page.

"Don't do that!" Gwen said. "Try another section. Here," she said, pointing to a corner of the page. "Just practice a bit. Like this." She took a big brush, expertly swiped a bit of water on the page, then dabbed a bit of dark paint into a pool of water on my palette. A moment later, a beautiful, transparent blue blossomed on the top of the page, looking like a fresh rain puddle. "See? It's easy."

"Right," I said skeptically, and picked up the brush. Whatever artistic talent was in the family had clearly passed me by.

"How's this?" asked Lorraine Lockhart, brandishing a beautiful wash of light blue.

"Oh, that's fabulous!" Gwen said. "I like how you managed the color gradation. Good job!"

I watched as Gwen walked around the room dispersing compliments. Maybe I should try one of the other classes, I thought as I dabbed at the paper yet again, making more unwieldy blue blotches. Three artists from the mainland were spending a few months in residency and were giving classes: a potter, an oil painter, and a sculptor who worked in wood, just like my husband. The potter was less than amazing—although he called his lumpish creations "an organic representation of life on the sea bottom," Gwen had told me privately that Chad Berman, their creator, was the son of one of the benefactors, and was really there more for the funding than the talent. On the other hand, Emma Frisch, the artist who worked in oils, had done some close-ups of local flora that made me think of her as a modern Georgia O'Keeffe, and the sculptor, a woman named Thuy Nguyen, from my hometown of Austin, was a master of wood carving. John had really enjoyed having a colleague to share tips and experience with; I was already seeing some new techniques emerging in his gorgeous driftwood sculptures.

"I'm not sure I'm cut out for this," Charlene said as she held up her paper for examination. Dribbles of paint rolled down to the bottom. "Oops."

"There are no mistakes," Gwen crooned. "Only opportunities!"

"Opportunity my patootie. If this were red, it would look like a murder scene," Charlene observed under her breath. "And speaking of murder and other violent acts," she added brightly, "did you hear what happened down at the co-op yesterday?"

"Do I want to know?"

"Mac Penney drank too much and rammed Earl Randall's boat."

"What? That's crazy. Why?"

"I'm not sure if it was drink or something else, but it's going to take a week or so for Eli White to fix it. Earl is lucky it didn't sink."

"It wasn't an accident," Lorraine said.

"Earl accused Mac of hauling his traps last week," Charlene informed me.

"Tom told me about that," Lorraine pitched in. "A lot of locals have been light on lobsters, but Mac keeps hauling in more than his share. There's been some talk that maybe he's fishing extra traps."

"Anything to it?" I asked.

Lorraine grimaced. "I don't know if it's someone on the island or not, but someone's raiding other people's traps. And Adam accidentally hauled up an unmarked trap the other day... and it was connected to four more."

"That's seriously illegal," Charlene said. "Any idea who's doing it?"

Lorraine shook her head. "Mac is pretty sure Earl called the Marine Patrol on him, though."

"Why does he think that?" I asked.

"There's an observer coming to the island tomorrow. She's asked to go on Mac's boat."

"I think she's booked at the inn," I said. Because the Gray Whale Inn was the only place to stay on Cranberry Island, it made sense that the guest I had arriving tomorrow must be the observer in question; her name was Chelsea Sanchez, and she'd booked for a week.

"Maybe you can find out why she's really here," Charlene suggested. "Mac thinks it's because Earl said traps are being hauled illegally; he thinks she's an investigator, not just an observer."

Lorraine twirled her paintbrush in the air and leaned in toward us. "Mac had a few PBRs to drown his sorrows, and when he ran into Earl at the co-op, he threatened to make him lose his license... or worse."

"That doesn't sound good."

"I know," Lorraine said, "and Tom's worried things are escalating. You heard what happened on Matinicus a few years ago, right?"

"I know it's an island down the coast, but I don't know anything else. Fill me in."

"There was a horrible gear war," Lorraine said.

Charlene waved her paintbrush. "I remember that. It ended in more than a quarter-million dollars in damages, right? And didn't some guy's boat get torched, like three times?" Charlene asked.

"Exactly," Lorraine said.

"You don't really think we're going there, do you?" I asked. We'd had troubles a few years ago with folks from off island intruding on the traditional fishing grounds—although the lines aren't "official," they were fiercely guarded—-but things seemed to have settled down. At least until now.

"Someone's been hauling other people's traps," Lorraine said. "We don't know who it is. There's been some talk of doing surveillance, but you can't just put a camera on someone's boat without telling them about it."

"I remember there was some talk in the legislature about changing that a few years ago, but it got voted down," I said.

"It did," Lorraine confirmed. "The Marine Patrol has to give anyone twenty-four hours' notice before installing surveillance equipment."

"And who would be stupid enough to do something illegal on camera?" Charlene asked.

Lorraine's mouth quirked up in a smile. "You might be surprised. But generally, people do behave better when they're being filmed."

"Well, if this keeps up, Eli will have plenty of work lined up this coming winter," Charlene pointed out. "Speaking of Eli, he seemed a little worried when I saw him yesterday."

"What's up?"

"Claudette's last checkup didn't go so well, apparently. A couple of weeks ago, he told me they want her to go in for more testing." That was not news I wanted to hear—not at all. Claudette and Eli White were pillars of the island. Claudette was a fierce protector of island habitat and had always been active in island affairs... despite the fact that her two goats, Muffin and Pudge, had been the terrors of local gardens for years. She'd reconnected with her long-lost son and his young family not too long ago, and she and Eli were savoring the experience of being parents—and grandparents—for the first time.

"Oh, no," I said. "Diabetes?" I knew she'd been prediabetic for some time; everything she baked was sugar-free, so I often slipped her husband a few extra cookies from the inn. It was our little secret.

"No. Something else. I don't know the details, but Eli didn't look so good."

"I'll have to swing by to check on him," I said.

Charlene looked worried. "Me too. I hope she's going to be okay."

As she spoke, Gwen drifted back over. "How's it going over here, ladies?"

"We got distracted," I confessed. "I'll try again."

"It just takes practice," Gwen said as I smeared more blue water on the page. "You'll get it, Aunt Nat!"

"Right," I said, not feeling convinced.

That was okay, I told myself as I made yet another attempt to create something other than a blob on the page. Unfortunately, my next effort looked no better than the previous two.

I sighed and turned over the paper. Art class, so far, was not proving to be the calming distraction I'd hoped it would be.

On the plus side, at least I knew how to make a killer coffee cake.

WHEN CHARLENE and I stepped out of the Art Guild an hour later, the spring day was cool and fresh. Daffodils were blooming in the grass near the end of the drive, and a few small apple trees had unfurled their blossoms, perfuming the air with their sweet scent. I knew Fernand had planted the apple trees, and felt a twinge of sadness thinking of my lost friend. He'd been Gwen's mentor and had lived here and run a small art school before he'd been taken from us, far too soon. I still missed him, and was glad my niece was carrying on his legacy.

"Are you going by Eli and Claudette's?" Charlene asked as we turned right on Seal Point Road.

"I thought I might," I said. "I don't have that many guests at the inn right now, so the workload is light."

"I heard the woman who's renovating Cliffside is staying with you," Charlene commented. "What do you think of her?"

"She seems nice enough," I said. Sarah Greenwich had reserved a room for two weeks as she organized work on Cliffside, a big house that overlooked Cranberry Island's harbor and had been through many owners in the past several years. It was a pretty house, but for some reason, nobody could ever figure out what to do with it.

"Think she'll stick?"

"She seems excited about moving here," I said. "She used to summer on the island as a kid."

"Did she? What's her name?"

"Sarah Greenwich."

"It doesn't ring a bell," Charlene said. "I'll ask around. What's she doing to the place, anyway?"

"Just renovating the interior," I said. "Nothing grand."

"Not opening a rival B and B?"

"I hope not!" I said. "Bookings have been slow enough this spring. I don't need the competition."

"I'm sure things will pick up," Charlene said.

"The economy's been kind of up and down lately; I think that may be why some of my regulars have been slow in booking." I sighed. "I'm probably going to have to do some marketing."

"Gwen's done a great job getting the word out about the Art Guild," Charlene said. She was right; not only had Gwen gathered together the contributors, but she'd organized the class schedule, gotten residents in, and started signing people up. "Maybe she can give you a hand. Heck... maybe you could do art retreat weekends this summer."

"That's a great idea!" I said. "Why didn't I think of that?"

"Between the two of you, you could really do well, I think."

"Thanks," I said as we rounded the corner and headed toward the Whites' house. The smell of balsam was in the air, and I caught the sound of a bleating goat. A moment later, we spotted Muffin and Pudge, who were chained—as usual—to a tire that was supposed to limit their range. Unfortunately—also as usual—the control method had proved unsuccessful, and the two goats were again ravaging local Selectman Ingrid Sorenson's rose bushes.

"They're a menace," Charlene commented.

"They are," I said. "But they're cute, and I love their owner, so I can live with them."

"I'm worried about her," Charlene said. "Come to think of it, I haven't seen her as much recently."

"Hopefully it was a false positive, whatever the test was, and it's just the remnants of the winter blues," I said as we approached the little house. It was tidy enough, but Eli's line of work was made obvious by the boats marooned in the slightly overgrown yard next door. The sound of hammering came from his workshop as we came closer.

"Probably Earl's boat," Charlene said. "I know they had to haul her out of the water so she didn't sink."

"I wonder if Lorraine's right about why Mac rammed her?"

"I don't know," Charlene said, "but things at the lobster co-op are not good. Tempers are high lately. Is Mercury in retrograde or something?"

"I have no idea," I said as we crossed the yard to Eliezer's workshop, which was in an open barn in the middle of the boat-dotted field.

My friend had put down his hammer and was examining the hull of a white lobster boat with a big gash on the port side, right near what looked like the waterline. Charlene was right; Earl was lucky it hadn't sunk. "Hey there, Eli!" I said as we stepped into the barn. The yard might be messy, but Eliezer's workshop was neat as a pin. The tops of the walls were pierced with windows that filled the space with light, and although the barn doors were open, the interior smelled strongly of fresh lumber and marine paint.

"Well, well, well," Eli said. He smiled, but it didn't make it to his eyes. He was a thin, wiry man, with bright eyes, calloused hands, and gray hair. I'd never met anyone so passionate about boats—he'd made his living as Cranberry Island's boatwright for almost half a century now—and had an impish nature that always made me smile. "How's your boat treating you?" he asked.

"Terrific as always," I said. My friend had built my little skiff and always inquired after it; I got the feeling his boats were like his children. "I hear there was a bit of a collision in the harbor."

"You could say that," he said, pointing to the hole in the hull of the boat, whose name, *Lucky Lady*, was stenciled in peeling black paint. "The *Lucky Lady* is pretty lucky, from the looks of it. I'm surprised both boats didn't go down."

"I heard it wasn't an accident."

"You're right about that," Eli said. "I was down by the co-op when it happened. He plowed right into her, yelling about him being a thief the whole time. It's a good thing we got her out of the water as fast as we did, or we'd be hauling her up off the bottom."

"No kidding," Charlene said, inspecting the ragged hole. "He's lucky no one called John to come arrest him."

"That he is," Eli agreed. "He's going to be out of the game for a while until I get this patched up.

"Is Earl pressing charges?"

"I haven't heard yet," he said. "I wouldn't be surprised. Some of the other lobstermen are helping him out by hauling his traps for him."

"Are they going to get in trouble for that?" I asked. It was illegal to haul a trap marked with a buoy that didn't match the one on your boat.

"They gave the Marine Patrol a call and explained what's what so they don't get nabbed for it."

"Yeah... they're probably going to be paying extra attention to Cranberry Island about now. What the heck is going on at the co-op?"

"Somebody's poaching," Eli said. "Sad to say, I think it's someone on the island; I haven't seen any boats I don't know prowling around, and nobody else has either."

"Any idea who?"

"Mac's had hard times lately," he said. "I think he's got some expensive habits."

"Like what?"

Eli shrugged and looked away. Charlene and I exchanged glances; I didn't pursue it.

"So Earl thinks he's poaching other people's traps because he's short on funds?"

"That's the theory," Eli said. "And he's not the only one who thinks it."

"Anyone else in trouble on the island that you know of?" I asked.

"What are you, an investigator?" Charlene asked, poking me in the arm.

"I just don't like it when things are riled up like this," I said. "How's Claudette? I heard she might have some testing to do."

The corners of Eli's mouth turned down. "She got some bad news at the doctor's yesterday," he said.

My stomach tightened. "Oh, no. What's wrong?"

"They're not a hundred percent sure yet," he told us, "but they think she might have cancer."

2

"Cancer?" Charlene breathed. "Oh, Eli... what kind?"

"They're thinking maybe lymphoma. I don't know yet," he said. "She's slowed down a bit, and is sleeping a lot more. Maybe if they start treatments..." He drifted off.

"We're here a hundred percent, whatever you need," I assured him, touching his arm.

"Thanks, Natalie," he replied, looking haunted. "I just don't know how we're going to tell the kids."

"You don't know for sure yet, though, right?"

"No," he said, his face drawn. "But I have a bad feeling."

I knew how that went. "Is Claudette here?" I asked.

"She was going to lie down when I came out to work after lunch," he said. "I'm sure she'd love a visit. Don't say anything about the tests, though, please. I don't know if she wants anyone to know."

Because I'd already heard about it through the grapevine, it looked like the cat was already out of the bag, but I simply nodded. "Of course."

Eli put down his tools and brushed off his hands. "Let's go look in on her, then." He looked at me with a mischievous glint in his eyes. "You didn't happen to bring any cookies, did you?"

I laughed. "Claudette would ride me out of town on a rail if I did!" I kept Eli supplied with treats by making deliveries to Charlene's store on a regular basis. Charlene sold—or ate—most of them, but I always set a few aside for Eli. "But I might be willing to drop off a few at the store for you tomorrow."

"The lemon kind?"

"I'm out of lemons, I'm afraid... but I'm planning to make a batch of scones I think you'll like."

"I could go for some of those about now," he said in a wistful tone of voice. "Only thing in the house right now is some kind of cake made with coconut flour and stevia." He made a face. "I'd rather just go hungry."

I laughed as we walked to the house together. "I'll whip some up today, I promise."

"Better make a double batch," Charlene suggested. "Those will sell like hotcakes down at the store. If I don't eat them all first." She groaned. "I'll never fit into my dress for the concert this weekend."

"What concert?"

"Robert's taking me to see a jazz band on MDI," Charlene said, blushing. I smiled; my cousin Robert had recently moved to Bangor, and ever since he and Charlene met at Gwen and Adam's wedding, they'd been seeing each other regularly. Charlene had had a string of bad luck with previous boyfriends. I was hoping this one would last a while.

"Tell him hi for me!" I said as Eli opened the front door of the house he shared with Claudette.

A basket of wool skeins sat on the table in the middle of the room. Although there was a project in progress—a blanket in vivid shades of blue and green—on the small table next to Claudette's favorite rocking chair, she was nowhere to be seen. I felt another twinge of misgiving; Claudette was always on the go.

"Claudie?" Eli called into the dim hallway leading back to the bedrooms. "Nat and Charlene are here to visit."

"They're here?" she called, her normally robust voice sounding thin. Charlene and I exchanged glances as she continued. "I'll be out in a few. Make them some tea, please!"

"Will do," Eli said, bustling into the kitchen to fill the tea kettle. Charlene and I settled ourselves at the kitchen table as Eli busied himself filling a plate with something that looked a little like dirt clods.

"What are those?" I asked.

"Date-coconut balls," he said, then gave me a meaningful glance. "Sugar-free."

"Ah," I said as he put the plate on the table. Charlene and I eyed it dubiously.

"You first," she murmured. I reached out and took one, then bit into it, expecting something horrible. To my surprise, it wasn't half bad. It wasn't something I'd be filling the cookie jar with, mind you, but the flavor of the dates and coconut was far better than I had anticipated, even if the texture was a bit gummy.

Charlene had just braved one when Claudette shuffled into the room, wearing a bathrobe and looking ten years older than the last time I'd seen her. Her face was drawn, and her hair, usually braided down her back, was flattened against the side of her head.

"It's so good to see you," I said, standing up and pulling out one of the kitchen chairs. She sat down slowly, as if in pain.

"I'm sorry I'm not more presentable," she said. "I'm sure you've heard."

"We know there's something going on medically," I admitted, "but we don't know the details."

She gave me a bleak look. "I don't either. At least not yet. But they think I might have lymphoma."

Behind her, there was a rattle as Eli dropped a cup.

"I'm so sorry, Claudette," I said, reaching out to squeeze her hand. She did look as if she'd lost a bit of weight; her normally round cheeks seemed hollower than I was used to seeing them. "When will they know?"

"They have to do a biopsy on my lymph node," she said. "It's the day after tomorrow. I'm sick with worry... I have no idea how I'm going to tell the kids."

"You'll figure it out," I said. "They love you. I'm sure they'll want to be with you as you go through this."

"But I don't want to worry them," she said.

"Wouldn't you want to know if it was someone you loved?" I said. "It's up to you, of course, but I think getting as much support as you can is a good thing."

She pursed her lips. "I don't know..."

"Speaking of support," Charlene said, "let's get dinners organized."

"But I don't want the whole island to know!" Claudette said.

"They don't have to," Charlene reassured her. "Nat and I will take care of it quietly. Now," she said, going into business mode, "I know you do sugar-free, but do you have any other restrictions?"

"Are you sure?" she asked.

"Positive," Charlene and I responded in unison.

Relief washed over her face. "I can't eat gluten," she said.

"Got it," I said. "Now, when and where's the procedure taking place?"

"The hospital on Mount Desert Island," she said. "Eli's taking me."

"Do you need company?" Charlene offered. "I can get Tania to cover that day, easily."

Claudette looked at her husband, who was quietly pouring hot water over the tea bags in the tea pot. "Do you want Charlene to come with us?"

"The company might be nice," he admitted.

"Then I'll schedule it," Charlene said firmly. "I'm so sorry you are having to go through this; the waiting is the hardest part, isn't it?"

"It is," Claudette said. "I knew I was more tired than usual... but lymphoma? A biopsy? I haven't slept more than two hours since they told me the news."

"Oh, Claudette," I said. "I understand, believe me. I'm a worrier."

"And there's no guarantee it's lymphoma or anything nasty," Eli pointed out as he pulled out four mugs from the cabinet. "You've had a cold for months. It could just be swollen nodes!"

"He's right," I said.

"I don't know, though," Claudette said. "The bloodwork..."

"Whatever it is, we're with you," I told her, squeezing her hand again. Charlene took her other hand, and our old friend looked at us both with tears in her eyes.

"Thank you," she said as her husband poured the tea.

≈

BY THE TIME WE LEFT, both Claudette and Eli were in better spirits, and we'd figured out a dinner plan for the next week.

"I hope it's just a false alarm," Charlene said as we turned at the end of the driveway, past the nodding daffodils. The scent of apple blossoms was on the breeze, and already the lupine plants were stretching toward the sun; it wouldn't be long before they burst into bloom. It was hard to reconcile the beauty of the day with my worry over our friend.

"Me too," I said. "She does look like she's not doing so hot, though. I'm worried."

"Yeah." Charlene kicked at a chunk of broken pavement; it landed among a patch of blueberries, their blossoms looking like little fairy skirts.

"Even if it's not a false alarm, though, they've made a lot of progress with cancer treatments. With any luck, it'll be something curable."

"Here's hoping," she said. Her eyes drifted over to the bashed-up lobster boat in Eli's workshop. "I have a bad feeling about how things are heating up down at the co-op."

"Me too," I said again. We'd asked Eli for details about the run-in, but he'd been kind of vague. "Did you get the feeling Eli knew more than he was saying?"

"I did." Her brow creased. "What could it be, though? Is he protecting someone?"

"I don't know," Charlene said. "But there's something fishy going on. I don't think we've seen the last of it all."

"No," I agreed. "And the observer is checking in tonight. I'm going to tell her to be careful."

"You really think someone would hurt an observer?"

"Tempers are high, and she's an outsider. I'd like to think not, but better safe than sorry."

We'd reached the fork in the road; to the left was the

store and Charlene's cottage, and to the right was the inn. I only had a few guests tonight, and plenty of food for dinner. "Want to come over to the inn tonight?" I asked. "Maybe we can get started prepping meals for Claudette and Eli. And you can tell me what you think of my scone recipe."

"Scone recipe?" Charlene asked.

"I'm entering my scones into a cooking contest this month," I said. "For the Portland paper. The prize money is only five hundred dollars, but I'm hoping to get some press if I win."

"What kind of scones?"

"I'm planning to make cherry, dark chocolate, and toasted hazelnut this afternoon," I told her.

"Three kinds of scones, or all of that in one scone?"

"All in one."

Charlene considered the offer. "Those do sound pretty amazing. I guess I don't have to go back to the store, and the ground beef I put in the fridge to thaw can keep for another day... and obviously you need testers."

"I do," I said. "Besides, this way we can meet the observer together. She's supposed to be in on the three o'clock mail boat."

"Maybe we can find out if she really is an observer, or a plant from the Marine Patrol... and if she knows anything we don't."

I grinned at my friend. "You and I both know that you'll find out everything by the end of tomorrow anyway."

Her lips quirked up into a smile. Thanks to her chatty nature and her position as island postmistress, not much escaped Charlene. "I do have my sources," she admitted.

WE GOT BACK to the inn about twenty minutes later. Charlene sat at my kitchen table as I rolled hazelnuts into a pan and tucked them into the oven to roast. As the intoxicating scent of roasting nuts filled the air, I grabbed butter from the fridge, opened the flour canister, and set to work on the dough.

"So tell me what you know about Mac Penney," I said.

"Other than that he's got a few screws loose?" She grinned and sat back in her chair. "He's been on the island forever... inherited his fishing license from his dad. He lost two fingers about ten years ago—got them trapped in the line as he was pulling it up—and almost drowned last year, but he's never done anything else in his life."

"Almost drowned?" I asked.

"He fell off his boat," she said. "Probably too much Pabst Blue Ribbon. He never learned how to swim. If his sternman hadn't managed to haul him out, he would have been a goner."

"He's got a problem with liquor, then?"

". Maybe. Or maybe something worse."

"Drugs?" I asked.

"I don't know... it's just a theory. There's been some talk that Mac's been playing fast and loose with the rules, maybe to support a habit."

"You mean he's fishing other people's traps?" I asked as I cut the butter into the flour.

"That's one rumor, but some folks think he's fishing with unmarked traps, too," she said.

"That's a big no-no, isn't it?" I'd educated myself on the lobstering culture—and regulations—since moving to Cranberry Island.

"It is," she confirmed. "No wonder he's not happy about the observer hanging out on his boat."

"I thought observers weren't associated with law enforcement," I commented as I pulled a carton of eggs from the refrigerator. I was getting low; I made a mental note to add them to my grocery list.

"They aren't," Charlene said. "They're part of some government agency. But I think he thinks she's undercover for law enforcement or something."

"Ah," I said. "But if lots of people are suspicious, why does he think Earl blew the whistle?"

"They've never gotten along," she told me. "They had some kind of feud when they were teenagers, and it's done nothing but get worse as the years have progressed."

"What's the feud about?" I asked.

"You know? It was so long ago, I don't even know," she said. "I'll have to ask around. But I know Earl was spreading rumors that he'd seen Mac hauling up Adam's traps. If it were only him, I'd question it, but Tom Lockhart mentioned that Mac and Adam have been bringing in more lobsters than anybody else lately. They both say they've just got good fishing spots, but everyone else is fishing the same territory, and everyone knows where their traps are; they're marked with buoys."

"Adam? I can't believe he'd do anything wrong." I didn't like to hear that my nephew-in-law might be involved. I pulled the pan of hazelnuts from the oven; they were a delightful golden brown, and smelled delicious. "They're getting the lobsters from somewhere," I said as I sampled one of the nuts and handed one to Charlene.

"Thanks," she said, crunching into the warm hazelnut. "Mmm. Anyway, someone's fishing either other people's traps or hidden traps, most likely. I also heard Mac might be scrubbing females and selling shorts to one of the pounds on Mount Desert Island."

"Wow," I said. Scrubbing females meant that instead of marking egg-bearing females, who carry their eggs on their bellies, with a V-notch and returning them to the water, he was dipping them in bleach and removing their eggs. And "short" lobsters were ones that hadn't yet reached a size where they could be sold legally. Maine lobstermen took conservation of the species seriously; both of these infractions were a very big deal. "How do they know a lobster's been scrubbed, anyway?" I wondered.

"I think they dip them in something that shows whether or not they've been exposed to bleach," she said. "I haven't seen anything about it in the *Daily Mail*, but I've heard one of the lobster pounds in Southwest Harbor may be under investigation. And I've heard rumors that Mac's boat has been tied up at the dock there a couple of times recently."

"Not the most reliable source," I pointed out as I grabbed a bar of Valrhona dark chocolate from the pantry and put it on the chopping board.

"True," she said. "It's a big mess right now. Nobody trusts anybody, and people are threatening to cut each other's gear."

"Who knew lobstering was so full of intrigue?" I said. "I can see why Mac is suspicious of the observer, though. Is anyone monitoring Adam?"

"Everyone's keeping an eye on everyone now," she said. "But if you're fishing unmarked traps, you find them with GPS and haul them at night, when no one's watching."

"You'd have to keep a constant watch on the harbor, then."

"You would," she said. "And some of the boats moor far enough out, it's hard to see them at night."

"One of the downsides of open water, I guess. Hard to monitor."

"It's a challenge," she admitted. "They tried to pass legislation to make covert surveillance an option a few years back, but it didn't go through."

"So it's still the Wild West out there."

"More or less," she said, sighing. "I'm just worried things may get out of hand."

People were already ramming into other boats, I reflected. How much worse could it get?

"I'm sure it'll all blow over," I said as I added the hazelnuts to the bowl of rich dark chocolate.

Unfortunately, it didn't blow over. And things were about to get worse than I ever imagined.

he scones were a smashing success; as we figured out our plan to feed Claudette and Eli for the week, both Charlene and I ate two each, slathered with clotted cream; with the cherries, they didn't need any jam.

"I have to stop," she groaned. "But these are amazing."

"I think this one may be a winner," I agreed. "I still have two more recipes to experiment with, though. So stay tuned."

"With pleasure," she said, licking her fingers. She glanced at the clock. "When is your observer supposed to show up, again?"

"Three," I told her.

"It's two forty-five now," she said. "Are you picking her up in the van?"

"She told me she'd rather walk. And it's a gorgeous day; I would, too."

"So no panic."

"And the rooms are clean," I said, "so I'm off-duty for a while."

"How are things now that Gwen's not here anymore?" she asked.

Since she and Adam had gotten married, they'd taken up residence at Adam's house. And now that Gwen was so busy getting the Art Guild up and running, she'd been at the inn a lot less frequently. "I miss her," I said. "And I'm still getting used to the extra work. I may have to hire someone to help out; Catherine, John, and I are handling it, but it would be nice to have a break. If I can get the occupancy up, I'm going to see if I can have Marge come back to help me out again."

"That sounds like a good plan," she said. "What are you doing to up bookings?"

"I'm sending out a newsletter tomorrow," I said. "And doing the contest, of course. I was thinking of putting together a cookbook, too."

"Oh, that's a great idea," she said. "You could call it *The Gray Whale Inn Kitchen*."

"I like it!" I told her. "You're full of good ideas."

"You really should talk to Gwen about it," she said. "She did some computer course on online marketing; I'm sure she'd be happy to help."

"I should," I said. As I spoke, my mother-in-law, Catherine, walked into the kitchen. Although she was normally decked out in cashmere and pearls—even when changing sheets in the guest rooms—today she was dressed down in a wool sweater I'd never seen before and a pair of trim-fitting but unusually faded jeans. And she wasn't wearing lipstick.

"Hey, Catherine."

"Hi," she said shortly.

"Is everything okay?" I asked.

"What do you mean?" she barked.

I blinked. "Your energy seems a bit off," I said, trying to be tactful. "I'm just checking in."

"I'm fine," she bit out. "Now, if you'll excuse me, I'm just going to switch the laundry and go lie down. I have a headache."

As Charlene and I stared at each other, Catherine marched into the laundry room. We could hear the sound of the washer door being slammed open and, a moment later, the dryer door shut with a clang and the machine start. She marched back into the kitchen and out the back door, a thin smile that resembled a grimace on her face.

When the door slammed shut, I turned to Charlene. "What was that about?"

"I don't know," Charlene said. "But I can guess."

"Oh? Do tell."

"Well, I heard Murray was spending a good bit of time up at Cliffside yesterday, talking with the new owner."

"Sarah Greenwich?"

"That's the one. And he was there the day before, too, giving his 'professional opinion.'" Charlene made air quotes, then took a sip of tea. "She's kind of pretty."

"She is," I agreed. I'd seen her at breakfast at the inn, and she had a sporty, zesty vibe to her that I could see could be very alluring. "And she's driven, too... kind of like Murray. Birds of a feather, in a way."

"Could be trouble."

"It could," I said. I'd seen Murray be jealous of Catherine, but this was the first inkling I'd had that it might go the other way around. "She's booked for another week at the inn," I said.

"And she's moving here permanently soon."

I sighed. "I never thought I'd say this, but I hope you're wrong and they're still solid. I've never liked Murray, but he seems to make Catherine very happy."

"It takes all kinds," Charlene said, then got a dreamy look on her face.

"What?" I asked.

"Oh, just thinking about Robert," she said. "He's just so amazing. He brings me flowers every time he comes to see me, and makes coffee before I wake up. Why did you keep him a secret all this time?"

"I didn't," I said. "Besides, he was living in Chicago, and I know how you feel about long-distance relationships." Charlene's last relationship with a freelance naturalist had died an early death when she realized she'd only see him four times a year.

"We kind of are long-distance," she pointed out. "He lives in Bangor."

"But he's here every weekend and you're on the phone all the time," I pointed out. As I spoke, her phone vibrated. She looked down at it and smiled. "Aw! He sent me a recipe for eggs Benedict. We're going to try it out this weekend."

I smiled. "I'm glad," I said. "You deserve some goodness in your life."

"I do, don't I?"

"We all do," I said, and my thoughts drifted to Claudette and Eli. I hoped the cancer scare was a false alarm. And that whatever was going on down at the co-op would settle down soon, so the island could return to its normal, peaceful atmosphere.

Hope springs eternal, I guess.

CHARLENE and I had just finished a third scone each when she spotted a solid figure in a red windbreaker trundling down the driveway to the inn, a green rolling suitcase bumping along behind her.

"Looks like your observer's here," Charlene said.

"I'm glad they let her get past the co-op without ripping her to shreds," I said.

"They probably didn't know who she was yet," Charlene said cheerily. "I hope she knows self-defense."

Charlene joined me as I walked to the front desk; a moment later, the front door opened, and the woman we'd seen coming down the driveway walked in, pulling her suitcase in after her.

"You must be Chelsea," I said. "Welcome to the Gray Whale Inn."

"Thanks," the young woman said, giving me an uncertain smile. There was a gap between her front teeth that somehow made her look younger than her years. She looked around the front hall, which featured my big cherry desk, cubbyholes for mail and keys, and a blue Oriental rug. "This is nice," she said. "So much better than a Motel 6."

"I hope so!" I said, handing her a key as she fished out a credit card. "I put you in the Rose Room, on the first floor; it's got a great view of the ocean. There are cookies in the dining room, along with coffee and tea, and we serve dinner if you're interested; otherwise, you can go to Spurrell's Lobster Pound, on the dock."

"Thanks," she said. "I'll probably run down to the Pound and get a cup of chowder; I had a big lunch. When's breakfast?"

"It starts at eight," I told her.

She grimaced. "I'm supposed to be at the dock at nine."

"You can eat fast and I'll run you over in the van. As for lunch, I'll put something together you can take with you," I said. "Any dietary restrictions?"

"I probably should have some," she said ruefully, "but I don't. I'm a sucker for baked goods."

I smiled at her. "Good, because those are my specialty. I'll put together a sandwich and toss in a few cookies and some fruit, if that works for you."

"That would be terrific," she said.

"We'll take care of you. First time on the island?" I asked as I ran her card.

"It is," she said.

"How long have you been working as an observer?" I asked. "It must be interesting work."

"It's not really," she said. "I get paid by the National Oceanic and Atmospheric Administration... NOAA. You sit on boats and count fish or lobsters," she said. "And a lot of the time, the people on the boat don't want you there." She sighed. "It's not ideal, but at least it's a paycheck."

"How did you get into that line of work?"

"I was a marine biology major," she said. "I wanted to do something related. I'm thinking I may have to go back to grad school, though. I'm not sure yet."

She looked to be about twenty-five, I gauged. If she was an undercover Marine Patrol officer, she had a very convincing cover story. "I hear you're going out on Mac Penney's boat."

"How did you know?"

"It's a small island," I said. "He's not the friendliest, I'm afraid."

She sighed. "I always get the grouchy ones. It's all right. I'll just stay out of the way as much as I can."

"Good plan," I said as I handed her back her card. "I'll have everything ready for you in the morning."

"Thanks," she said. "Wish me luck!"

I did. I felt bad for anyone who had to spend a full day at sea on Mac's boat. I hoped she was up to it.

"I don't think she's working undercover for the Marine Patrol," I told Charlene once I heard the door of the Rose Room close.

"Me neither," she said.

I grimaced. "And boy, that poor young woman's got some fun ahead of her."

"Of all the lobster boats on all the islands..."

"If he is indulging in too much liquor, or something else, I hope he's okay to operate a boat," I said thoughtfully. "It could be dangerous."

"On the plus side, he's less likely to ram into other people's boats with an observer on board," Charlene pointed out.

"True. Evidently, he didn't do much damage to his own vessel; Eli didn't say anything about it, and Earl's was the only one in the boat barn."

"He got lucky," she said. "Anyway, she'll have to figure it out. I'm sure he'll be on his best behavior."

"That's not saying much," I said.

I had a bad feeling about Chelsea Sanchez's arrival on the island. Things were already simmering down at the co-op. I was afraid her presence would turn up the heat so much that things might boil over.

Unfortunately, I wasn't wrong.

I SENT some of the scones back with Charlene, asking her to earmark a few for Eli, and then set to work prepping dinner. It was only the two of us tonight; none of the guests were eating in, and Catherine was fending for herself. I hadn't seen Sarah all day; I imagined she was over on the main-land, picking out appliances or organizing contractors. Once I'd finished making the marinade for the flank steak I was cooking, sliced the potatoes and tossed them with olive oil, salt, and a touch of rosemary, and whipped up a vinaigrette dressing for the salad, I busied myself working on the news-letter. As the flank steak marinated, I wrote about the apple blossoms starting to perfume the island, the lupines that were just beginning to unfurl, the recipes I was working on —I included one of my perennial favorites, a sausage, egg, and cheese strata that was always a hit—and some of the upcoming events around the island. I also put in a referral special and added a paragraph about our "romantic getaway weekend packages," which included a bottle of champagne, chocolates, a candlelit dinner, and the nicest suites in the inn. Gwen had suggested the idea a few months earlier, but I hadn't gotten around to putting it together; I'd have to update the website soon.

There was always more to learn when you had a small business, I thought as I put the finishing touches on the draft, including a few pictures of the inn and one of Smudge, our most recent feline addition, drowsing on the back porch. I really did need to talk to Gwen about setting up some kind of co-op retreat with the new Art Guild. There was the revenue from John's art, so our situation wasn't dire, but with Gwen moving out, even with Catherine and John pitching in, I was short on help, and we didn't have much in the budget to pay for it. I'd considered offering room and board to a potential employee, with reduced salary to compensate, but I wasn't sure how comfortable I'd be having a stranger living in our private quarters and sitting across the kitchen table from us every morning and evening.

It would all work itself out, I told myself as I closed up

the laptop and headed back to the kitchen, where I assembled the salad and headed to the back porch to start up the grill. Then I busied myself whipping up a lasagna to take to Claudette and Eli, and managed—for a little while—to forget about all of my problems.

I WAS SURPRISED to see Catherine in the kitchen when I came down the next morning at seven to get ready for breakfast. Unlike yesterday, this morning she in a twinset and slacks that showed off her trim figure and her makeup was impeccable.

I smiled at my mother-in-law. "You're up early," I said, pulling back my hair into a tie and heading for the coffee maker.

"I just thought I'd give you a hand this morning," she said. Since this had never before happened, I didn't quite know what to say, but I was guessing it had to do with whatever might be happening between Murray and Sarah Greenwich, who would likely be down for breakfast in the dining room.

"All right," I said. "I was planning on making apple puff pancakes; the recipe is at the end of the counter, if you'd like to do that."

She made a face. "You know I'm horrible at baking."

"All right, then," I said. "You can cut up some fruit, then. And make a roast beef sandwich for a box lunch, if you don't mind."

"But what about my clothes?"

"There's an apron on the hook," I said, pointing to the door to the laundry room. Catherine, I was concluding yet again, was far more help cleaning rooms than helping out in the kitchen. "There are strawberries and a cantaloupe in the fridge."

"No blueberries?"

"It's early for blueberries still," I reminded her.

"Oh." She picked a flowered apron from the hook, tied it around her waist, and retrieved the fruit from the refrigerator. As I gathered the ingredients for the apple puff pancake recipe—lots of eggs, and only a little bit of flour, oddly enough—Catherine sliced the cantaloupe in half and began scooping out the seeds.

"How are things going?" I asked tentatively as I mixed flour, baking powder, and salt into a large bowl. The volume of the pancakes relied on whipping egg whites, which I'd have to do at the last minute. Getting everything else ready now—and leaving the egg whites to warm to room temperature, which meant better whipping later—would make it easier to get the pancakes to the table when my guests arrived.

"Fine," she said quickly. "Why?"

"You just seem a little on edge," I said.

"The whole island's on edge," she pointed out.

"I know," I said. As I cracked an egg and separated it, I asked, "Have you heard anything about what's going on at the co-op?"

"Well, I heard about the boat accident," she said. "And I heard someone from the Marine Patrol is going undercover to figure things out."

"I think you're talking about the observer who checked in yesterday," I said. "She didn't strike me as an undercover officer at all; it could just be a rumor. Who did you hear it from?" I asked.

"Murray heard it from Tom Lockhart down at the store last weekend," she said.

"Ah," I replied, cracking another egg. "What does Murray think about what's going on at Cliffside?"

"He's spending a lot of time over there," Catherine said. "It's like he wants to be a free general contractor or something. I even saw paint swatches on the kitchen table yesterday."

"That sounds a little too close for comfort," I observed mildly, hoping I wouldn't set off a defensive response. I cared about Catherine. I wanted her to be able to talk to me.

"It does," she said shortly. Her slim shoulders slumped as she hulled a strawberry. "I know Murray and I have had our ups and downs, but I was starting to think that maybe... well, that Murray might be the one. And now all I hear about is Sarah and what's going on at Cliffside."

"That's hard," I said.

"And if she moves here, I'll never hear the end of it," she said. "It's funny. You finally let your guard down with someone, and then something like this happens."

"What do you know about her?" I asked. "Maybe they're just friends?"

"She was an investment banker in New York," she said. "They're both in to making money, markets, capital... all that stuff I don't know anything about."

"Maybe it's just a colleague thing," I suggested. "Not too many people around here know much about that stuff."

"Maybe," she said, "but my instinct tells me there's more to it than that."

"I get it," I said. "I hope you're wrong."

"Me too," she said, whacking off the top of a strawberry as if it were Sarah's head.

4

The first puffy apple pancake was ready right on schedule; I had also cooked up a pan of sausage links, and Catherine had assembled a fruit salad before pacing the kitchen for another hour. The guests all came down right as breakfast started, and settled into the tables by the windows.

Emma Frisch and Chad Berman, the two artists from the new guild staying at the inn, sat together at one table. Emma, who wore a gauzy top and harem pants and looked as if she had just flown in from another, more magical dimension, was sketching one of the roses in a vase on the table in her sketchbook and sipping a cup of coffee, while Chad, whose blond hair was twisted into dreadlocks, wore a fisherman's sweater, a pair of expensive-looking faded jeans, and a bracelet made of rope, chatted away at her. He seemed completely unaware that she was lost in her own world. Thuy, the wood sculptor who was working with John, sat alone at a table by the window, gazing out at the water. At another table was Sarah. She was very different from my mother-in-law, at least in appearance; where Catherine's hair was soft and blonde around her face, Sarah wore hers in a salt-and-pepper bob that accented her strong jawline; where Catherine had a refined look, Sarah's appearance was bold. She reminded me a little bit of a hawk somehow. At the moment, she had laid out architectural plans and was frowning at two wood samples.

The last table, off in the corner, was occupied by a couple, Noelle Sullivan and Bruce Pinkham, who were practically attached physically; her hand was on his thigh, and he kept stroking her, her back, her neck... I smiled. They were obviously very much in love. I kept forgetting they were at the inn because they spent so much time in their room.

As I filled everyone's coffee cup and let them know I'd have breakfast out in a moment, Chelsea hurried into the room, pulling on her red windbreaker. "Good morning! When's breakfast?"

"Right now," I said. "I'll bring yours out, along with your lunch. Want some coffee?"

"I'd love some," she said. As she sat down and I filled her cup, her eyes swept the room. She drew in her breath.

"What is it?" I asked. Her eyes were fixed on the other end of the room. "Oh... nothing," she said, but it didn't sound like nothing.

"Chelsea?" It was Chad, standing up and squinting at her. "Is that you?"

She swallowed hard. "Oh. Chad. I didn't see you there."

"What are you doing up here?" he asked, crossing the room.

"I work for NOAA," she said with a smile that didn't reach her eyes. "I'm going out on a lobster boat this morning; I'm an observer."

"Not painting anymore, then?" he asked.

"I still do some on the side, but I needed a job," she said, her face reddening. "I don't have a trust fund," she added bitterly, a jab that surprised me.

"My art supports me," he said, drawing himself up.

"Uh-huh. Must be nice," she said in a flat voice.

"Anyway," he said, obviously embarrassed, "I just wanted to say hi."

"Hi," she said, then turned to me. "Actually, can I get my breakfast to go? I think I'm going to walk over, and I don't want to be late."

"Sure," I said. "I'll pack it up; I'll be right back."

As I walked to the kitchen, I scanned the dining room. The lovebirds had withdrawn from each other; Noelle's hair cloaked her face, and Bruce had left the room. A lovers' quarrel? I wondered as I retreated to the kitchen to pack breakfast for Chelsea, who had left the dining room to wait in the parlor.

"Is she there?" Catherine asked when I walked into the kitchen.

"Sarah? She is," I said. "I need to pack a breakfast to go for Chelsea," I said, retrieving a box from the pantry and cutting a wedge of apple pancake.

"Is she running late?"

"She had a bit of a run-in with one of the artists from the Guild," I said. "She accused him of being a trust-fund baby, and that's when she decided to get breakfast to go."

"Well, he is a trust-fund baby," she pointed out. "His parents are half the reason the Guild is in business. They're hoping it'll give their son some kind of direction."

"I'd heard his parents were benefactors," I said, "but I didn't know the rest of it." I'd been unimpressed by his pottery offerings, but had decided it must just be that I wasn't up on modern art. "On the plus side," I said, "I no longer have to give her a ride to the dock; she's decided to walk."

"Good day for it at least," Catherine said, glancing out at the bright blue sky. She sighed. "I sometimes think it's a mixed blessing to be born into wealth," Catherine said. "Less worry about ending up homeless, of course, but if you're not motivated to make it big, I don't think you're as likely to work hard and go after your dreams..."

"He says he's supporting himself from his art," I said as I slid a slice of pancake into a box.

"That's a stretch," Catherine said. "Murray knows his parents. He's got an allowance of four thousand a month."

"That would help," I said. "Still... I wish him the best. It's hard being young."

"It's hard being any age," Catherine pointed out. "Mind if I serve breakfast?"

"Go ahead," I said. "Just don't bite her head off."

"I won't," she promised. "I'm just curious." Her tone was light, but she looked miserable. I hoped I was right, and it was just a friendship that had sprung up between Murray and Sarah, and not something more.

CHELSEA HAD DEPARTED, the rest of the guests had all been served, and I was dishing up a piece of puff pancake for myself when Catherine burst back through the swinging door. "He's here," she announced.

"Who?"

"Murray. He came to have breakfast with her!" She twisted the pearls at her neck so hard, I was afraid the strand would break. "She lit up like a Christmas tree when he walked in. And now I have to refill their coffee while they chat away about baseboards and the real estate market and..." She turned away and dabbed her eyes.

"I'll take care of it," I said. "Go have a piece of pancake."

"Too many carbs," she said reflexively.

"Fine. There's sausage in the pan. Let me go deal with them."

She looked up at me, her blue eyes red and puffy. "Tell me if you think I'm imagining things. Okay?"

"I'll do my best to get a feel for it," I said as I added some fruit salad and sausage to the plate I had been fixing for myself, then ferried it out to the dining room.

The rest of the guests were long gone, but Murray and Sarah had their heads bent over Sarah's blueprints and were talking excitedly, oblivious to me until I set the plate down on the table.

"Oh," Murray said, looking up in surprise. "Is that for me?"

"It is," I said.

"Thanks!" he told me. "You should see what Sarah has in mind for Cliffside. It's going to be gorgeous."

"Oh, Murray," she said, playing with the pendant at her throat. "It's just a simple renovation."

"No," he said. "You're really restoring it to its former glory.... It'll be a showplace when you're done with it. I wish you could have helped me when I was working on my place. You're so talented!"

"It's just all those years of renovating properties," she said. "Experience, not talent."

"Whatever it is, it's working. Maybe we should talk about flipping properties over on the mainland. I've got an in with a real estate agent over there, and with your know-how..."

She laughed. "I'm out of that business. Remember?"

"Oh, come on. It could be fun!" he said.

Sarah flipped her hair with her fingers. "I'll think about it. But for now, tell me what you think of these front-door options. I'm leaning toward the simpler one..."

I refilled their coffee as they pored over the plans, then returned to the kitchen to a waiting Catherine.

"Well?"

"They're talking about the plans," I said. "And about maybe going into business together."

"So it's all business?" she asked. "Did he ask why I wasn't the one in the dining room?"

"They were talking about doors," I said, trying to be kind. "I think they were distracted."

"So I don't have anything to worry about?"

I hesitated. I didn't want to stress Catherine out, but I didn't want to lie either. There had been chemistry in the dining room. Whether it was the excitement of a potential business partner or something more, I couldn't say for sure, but my instincts told me the attraction extended beyond real estate.

"I don't know," I said. "They do seem chummy."

Catherine deflated. "I knew it." She pushed her plate away, the solitary sausage link untouched. "I wish she'd never come to the island. As soon as they met, down at the dock, I knew there was going to be trouble."

"Don't jump to conclusions," I said. "Have you talked to him?"

She shrugged.

"You should. Besides, you're a catch. Don't forget that."

Catherine grimaced. "I didn't build my own financial empire."

"That could be in your favor, actually," I said. It was hard to believe I was encouraging Catherine not to give up on Murray Selfridge. The developer had an ego the size of the

Gulf of Maine, and had attempted to bully the board of selectmen to renovate the island to his liking more times than I could count, but since he'd met Catherine, I'd seen his softer side. Besides, with two potential real estate moguls teaming up, it couldn't be good for Cranberry Island. "Too many chiefs, you know?"

"That's true," she said. "I guess we just have to wait and see."

"Exactly," I said. "In the meantime, do you have things to keep you busy?"

"I'm supposed to take a pottery class down at the Art Guild," she said. "It starts this afternoon, but to be honest, I just don't feel up to it."

"Do it anyway," I said, even though I wasn't sure how much she'd get out of it if Chad was teaching it. "Any plans to see Murray?"

"We're supposed to go out on his yacht sometime in the next few days," she said. "Unless he cancels."

"I'm sure he won't," I said. "If I were you, I'd just throw myself into something absorbing." I grinned. "If you're up for a deep clean, I wouldn't object."

"I thought you said absorbing," she said with a glimmer of her normal spunky self.

"Seriously, though," I said. "I need to do some promotion to get reservations up for the summer. If you could help me brainstorm, or put some ads together, that would be great."

She sighed. "It's something, I guess."

"Maybe later this afternoon, then? After class?"

"Sure," she said in a lackluster voice. "It's better than staking out Cliffside, I suppose."

∼

I'D JUST FINISHED CLEANING up from breakfast when a call came from Tom Lockhart.

I closed the dishwasher with my hip as I picked up the phone. "Hey, Tom. What's up?"

"Have you seen Chelsea Sanchez?"

"Not since breakfast," I said, turning on the dishwasher. "Why?"

"Well, she never showed up at Mac's boat, apparently," he said. "Are you sure she didn't come back to the inn? Maybe she wasn't feeling well."

"I'll check," I said, and headed down the hallway to the Rose Room. I knocked and called her name, but there was no answer. I hurried back to the phone. "She's not answering, Tom. And I haven't seen her come back. That's a long time to be lost."

"I know," he said. "Someone cut free half the boats on the island last night, too. Mac's was one of them."

"Maybe she got there and realized there wasn't a boat to go on, and then went off-island?" I suggested.

"She wasn't on the mail boat," he said. "I called and asked."

I swallowed. "You don't think..."

"I hope there's a reasonable explanation," he said.

"Like maybe she went out on the wrong boat," I suggested.

"I already radioed," he replied. "She's not on board any of ours. Besides, they're all out looking for the missing boats."

"Find them?"

"We're still missing five," he said. "Adam's is one of them."

"Oh, no," I breathed.

"I don't want to call the authorities without good reason, but with the boats and the missing observer..."

My stomach tightened. "I'll knock again, and if she doesn't answer, I'll go in to look."

"I've got a call on the other line; maybe that's her. Let me know, okay?"

"I will," I promised, hanging up the phone and grabbing a key ring from the laundry room and hoping she was in her room.

Unfortunately, she wasn't.

he bed in the Rose Room was crisply made, and the few clothes Chelsea had brought hung in a neat line in the closet. Practical things, mainly... jeans, long-sleeved T-shirts, and sweatshirts. A pair of sneakers was lined up on the floor next to the bed, and there were two books on the nightstand: a self-help book I recognized called *The Slight Edge*, and a biography of Georgia O'Keeffe. To my surprise, there was a portable easel on the desk by the window, along with a small travel watercolor palette. An open sketchbook showed a sparse study of the view from the window. It was only a few brushstrokes, but the scene outside seemed to come alive on the page. Her style was different from Gwen's—sparer but evocative. I could almost see the movement of the water against the rocks by the shore, and the edge of the dock was a dark relief to the translucent green of the bank.

I didn't look further, as I didn't want to intrude, but after a quick check of the bathroom—there was a bottle of all-in-one shampoo on the side of the tub, but no sign of Chelsea —I hurried back to the kitchen to call Tom back.

He picked up on the second ring.

"She's not here," I said.

He cursed under his breath. "I hope we find her. If we don't..."

I understood. Not only was I worried about the young observer, but if a member of the co-op had sabotaged her, or worse...

"Let's not think about that yet," I said. "I'll tell John. It's a little early, but the circumstances are definitely odd. Maybe we should put together an island-wide search with whoever's not out on the water; John and I can start along the cliff trail. She wouldn't be the first one to trip."

"Good idea," he said. "Maybe she fell and hit her head," he added, sounding almost hopeful. Did he really think one of the lobstermen might have tossed her overboard? I wondered. How bad were things down at the co-op, really?

JOHN WAS busy sanding a piece of driftwood in his workshop when I knocked on the door a few minutes later.

"Hey," he said, giving me a bright smile. His face was coated with sawdust, but I didn't mind. "How was breakfast?"

"It went well—there's extra puff pancake in the fridge if you're hungry—but half the fleet had their mooring lines cut last night, and the observer went missing this morning."

He set down the piece of wood. "What do you mean, missing? Like, she-fell-off-a-boat missing?"

"I seem to be the last person who saw her, best I can tell. I gave her breakfast to go and a box lunch right after eight. She was going to walk down to the dock and meet Mac at nine, but he says she never showed up. His boat is missing anyway. And apparently, she's not on anyone else's boat; Tom radioed."

"And she didn't come back?"

"I checked her room," I said. "No sign of her. Tom's going to organize a search. He's already checked the main road, and there's no sign of her. I told him we'd check the cliff path together."

He sighed. "Guess it's a nice day for a walk, at least," he said. "I hope she just took a wrong turn, but it does seem like a long time to be lost on a small island."

"That's what I was thinking. I think Tom's worried someone might have done something to her."

John grimaced. "A lot of folks think she's here undercover for the Marine Patrol. I guess it's possible, but I hate to think that one of ours would do something like that."

"Someone may have thought there was a lot at stake," I suggested.

"Why would anyone cut all the boats loose?" he asked.

I had an idea why, but I didn't want to entertain it yet. "Let's focus on finding Chelsea first," I said. "It's not an ideal reason to play hooky and take a morning walk, but at least the weather's good. I'll go get my windbreaker. Need anything from the inn?"

"If you'd grab mine, that would be great. I have my phone here," he said, patting his pocket. "I was supposed to meet Thuy this afternoon, but that may have to wait."

"Let's hope not," I said.

I hurried back up to the inn, stopping in at the carriage house to tell Catherine what was up and ask if she'd seen any sign of Chelsea.

"Not since breakfast," she said, shaking her head. "Want me to take care of the rooms while you're out looking? If she shows up or calls, I'll let you know."

"That would be great," I said. "I have no idea how long we'll be gone; if we don't find her, we'll have to put together some kind of search party."

"I hope it doesn't come to that," she said. She looked lighter, I realized. "Things going better for you?" I asked.

"Murray stopped by to ask me to dinner," she said. "We're going after my pottery class."

"Oh, wonderful!" I told her. "I hope both go great."

"Me too," she said. "When you get back, maybe you can help me figure out what to wear tonight."

I blinked. This was the first time in history John's mother had ever solicited my opinion on anything of a sartorial nature. I resisted the urge to check her forehead for fever and simply said, "I'd be happy to. I'll let you know when we make it back. Thanks again for taking care of the rooms."

"Of course," she said, then hesitated. "Should I leave the Rose Room be? Just in case?"

I hated to even think it, but she was right. "Yes, please," I said. "I went in looking for her this morning anyway, and she's already made the bed and everything, so it'll be fine."

"Just checking," she said, but the question still needled me as I walked up the path to the inn. The breezy salt air was perfumed with the rich, winy scent of beach roses and the window boxes glowed with jewel-like nasturtiums and pansies, but this morning the inn's charms couldn't dispel the worry that was collecting in Chelsea Sanchez's absence.

I grabbed our windbreakers from the hook inside the kitchen and gave Smudge and Biscuit, who were curled up together in a sunbeam on the floor by one of the windows, a quick pet, then headed down to meet John.

He gave me a quick, sawdust-speckled kiss as I handed

him his windbreaker, and together we headed up the narrow path that led to the cliffs.

"The lupines are really going to be terrific this year, aren't they?" he said as we passed a swathe of the pink and purple flowers. They reminded me of bluebonnets on steroids. They might say everything's bigger in Texas, but they're wrong; where cheery bluebonnets are under a foot tall, some lupines extend to five feet or more. I loved them both. "Thuy is thinking of trying to sculpt some in wood; the shapes are really intricate."

"Flowers seem to be the theme of the Art Guild this spring, don't they?"

"Well, except for Chad," he said.

"What are Chad's... er... creations supposed to be, anyway?"

"Organic sea life forms," he said.

"Like sea urchins once their shells have been cracked and they've oozed out?"

"Something like that," John said. "He's working on it," he added charitably.

"I wonder how many people will take his class," I said as I stepped over a few wild strawberry plants. The little green plants had white flowers I knew would soon be bright red gems that were tart and sweet... perfect for trailside picking.

"My mother's going," he said.

"She told me about that. I hope she's kind."

"My mother is the soul of charity," John protested. My eyes slid over to him. "Mostly."

"She did ask me to help her pick an outfit," I said, "so there's that."

"Really?" he said. "For what?"

"Murray asked her to dinner tonight. She sounded unusually excited."

John sighed. "Sarah told me she was invited to an event on the island tonight."

"You think that's why Murray asked Catherine out?"

"I hate to think it, but maybe," he admitted. "She's nice enough, but I kind of wish Sarah would go back where she came from."

"Me too. Your mother and Murray seem to have a good thing going. I don't want it messed up."

John glanced at me. "Weird, isn't it? That we're rooting for Murray?"

"Yeah," I agreed. "But it's true."

We'd made it to the top of the hill. Although the view over the cliffs was magical, with the dark blue sweep of water dotted with buoys and the granite humps of the mainland mountains in the distance, so far, there had been no sign of Chelsea.

"We should probably check the cliff," John said grimly.

"We probably should." We'd found bodies there before, but I hoped today wouldn't turn up another one.

As we rounded a bend, John stepped over toward the cliff, scanning the beach at the bottom. "I don't see anything," he said, relief in his voice.

But I wasn't relieved at all. Ahead of us on the trail, tucked halfway under a blueberry bush, was a red windbreaker.

6

"Oh, no," I breathed, running over to where Chelsea lay, her legs sprawled across the trail. Her eyes were half-open, and her chest was still, the lunch box I'd packed for her crushed beneath her right arm. I could see a corner of the sandwich I'd made her just that morning. Unless I was wrong, she'd never get a chance to eat it.

John was right behind me. He felt her wrist for a pulse, and grimaced. "She's gone."

"How?" I asked.

He pointed; I hadn't noticed before, but her black hair was clumped, and the dirt beneath her head was stained dark.

"That's horrible," I said as John pulled out his cell phone and frowned at it.

"Bad reception," he informed me. "I'll stay here. Will you go back to the inn and call the police on the mainland?"

"Of course," I said. "You're sure she's gone?"

"No pulse, and she's cold. She's not breathing, either."

"Do you think maybe she fell and hit her head?"

"She's face-first, and the wound is on the back of her

head," he said. "It's possible, but I doubt it." He scanned the ground and pointed to a blood-spattered rock a few feet off the path.

"So someone..."

"It looks like it," he said grimly.

I looked at the young woman's lifeless body. She'd been so full of life when she headed out the door that morning, it just didn't seem possible that she was gone. "She was so young. Who could have done this?"

"Unfortunately, just about anyone," he said. "We're out of sight here."

"Was someone waiting for her, I wonder, or did they follow her?" I asked. "Do you think maybe Mac came to get rid of her before she could find something on his boat?"

"Anything's possible," he said.

I sighed and stood up. "I'll go call the mainland. I'll be back in a few. Need anything?"

"Maybe another cup of coffee," he said. "I think we may be here for a while."

WHEN I HURRIED into the inn kitchen, Catherine was busy folding towels.

"What's wrong?" she asked.

"We found Chelsea," I said.

"Is she okay?"

"No." I told her what we'd found.

My mother-in-law put down the towel she was folding, and her face paled. "You don't think it's someone at the inn, do you?" she asked. "Like maybe that young man I'm supposed to take my pottery class from this afternoon?"

"I don't know," I said honestly.

"Although maybe I can ask him how he knows her," Catherine said, a pensive look on her face.

"I wouldn't if I were you," I warned her. "We don't know anything about him."

"So you do think he's a murderer!"

"I'll wait for the coroner's report to say for sure. But in the meantime, I don't want anything to happen to you."

"So should I skip the class?"

"Do you know anyone else who's going?" I asked.

She shook her head. "Not many people signed up."

"Maybe I'll go with you," I suggested. The last thing in the world I wanted to do was to learn to make clay lumps, but I didn't feel comfortable sending Catherine alone. And I wanted to tell Gwen to be careful, too.

"We can ask questions together," Catherine suggested, pulling me out of a rather morbid reverie.

"Right," I said, but I couldn't shake my lingering worry about Gwen. I'd call her right after I called the police, I decided.

"It's at three," she said, picking up a stack of towels and heading toward the guest rooms. "Are you going to join me, then?"

"Yes," I agreed, and she was smiling as she headed to finish up the rooms. I was already dialing as she left.

I told the police what had happened, and they agreed to send over a launch. I called Gwen next. "It's Aunt Natalie. You're not alone, are you?" I asked when she picked up.

"Thuy and Emma are here with me," she told me, sounding perplexed. "Why?"

"Chad and Chelsea had a bit of a tiff this morning at the inn, and now Chelsea's... well, she's dead."

"Dead?" Gwen breathed.

"It looks like it might be foul play. I'm not saying Chad is responsible, but... be careful. With everyone. I wouldn't be alone with anyone if you can help it until we figure out what's going on. By the way, is there still room in Chad's pottery class?"

"Lots of it," she said. "I'm having a hard time getting people excited about it, honestly."

"Can you sign me up to come this afternoon?"

"Giving up on watercolor already?"

"No... well, maybe. I'm just keeping Catherine company."

"That's good of you," she said. "In the meantime, I'll see if I can find out anything about Chad and Chelsea's history."

"Don't," I warned her. "I don't want anything to happen to you."

"Now I know how you feel when John tells you to stay out of things," she said.

"That's different."

"Is it?" she asked. "Anyway, I'll see you this afternoon. I'm sorry about Chelsea... but keep me posted, okay?"

"I will. And stay safe."

"Of course, Aunt Nat. I love you."

"Love you too, sweetheart," I said, and hung up a moment later, still feeling a nagging worry.

BY THE TIME the launch arrived at the inn's dock, John and I had finished our coffee, and dark clouds were rolling in off the Gulf of Maine.

"I hope they get what they need before it rains," I said.

"Me too," he said, staring at Chelsea's windbreaker. "I keep wondering who did this," he added in a contemplative tone.

"It doesn't look like an accident, does it?"

"No, it doesn't," he agreed. "Mac is an obvious option... but how would he have known she was walking to the pier from the inn?"

"How would anyone have known she was walking along the path?" I asked. "When she arrived, she came here on the road, not the path."

"If someone was watching the inn, they would have seen her," he mused. "Her windbreaker isn't exactly camouflage."

"Or if they were at the inn already," I pointed out. "Chad had a run-in with Chelsea at breakfast this morning, and most of the inn's rooms have a view of the path."

"What time did everyone leave the inn this morning?"

"I don't know," I said. "I was busy in the kitchen; maybe Catherine noticed."

"You told me Chelsea called Chad a trust-fund baby," John said. "I can see that being insulting, but it doesn't exactly sound like a motive for murder."

"No, but there might be more to the story. We do know that they knew each other. And that their relationship seemed... complicated."

"Mac still seems more of an obvious suspect," he commented. "Maybe he came over and watched the inn, waiting for her so he could kill her before she got to the pier. If he got rid of her on the boat, suspicion would immediately fall on him, even if she went overboard."

"I'd rather it not be someone at the inn, frankly," I replied. "And Mac did ram someone's boat recently, so we know he's not averse to violence."

"If he did kill her, do you think it's because he's fishing illegally and didn't want to be found out?"

"I have no idea," I said. "Might be worth talking to them about it." I nodded toward the three people hurrying up the path toward us.

The quiet, windswept path quickly became a bustling crime scene. John and I reported what we knew to the detective. She told us to close off Chelsea's room until investigators had a chance to go through it.

"We'll have to wait for the coroner's report, but do you know of anyone who might have wanted her out of the picture?" she asked.

"There's been a bit of trouble down at the co-op. She was supposed to observe on a lobster boat, and the captain was none too happy about it," I said. "He thought someone had called the Marine Patrol and sent an undercover investigator; he ended up ramming another lobsterman's boat this week."

"That sounds like a good place to start," she said. "What's his name?"

"Mac Penney," I supplied.

"His boat is the *Blue Angel*," John added. "She was supposed to meet him at the town pier at nine, but she never made it there."

"Evidently not," the detective said, looking down at the prone form of Chelsea. "She's young, too. It's a shame."

"It is," I agreed.

"Does Mac have a sternman?" she asked.

"Josie Barefoot helps him out," John said. "But she's not always with him. He sometimes goes out solo."

"That's kind of unusual. Why?"

"That's what a lot of folks at the co-op are wondering," John told her.

"I'll be sure to talk with both of them," she said, making a note. "How long was she a guest at the inn?"

"She arrived late yesterday," I told her.

"Did she have any contact with other guests that you know of?"

"She knew one," I said, relating her exchange with Chad Berman.

"Interesting." The detective made another note. "Do you know where I can find him?"

"He's at island's Art Guild," I said.

"I'LL GO talk to him there," she said. "Anyone else?"

"Not that I know of," I told her.

"We'll have to interview your guests, I'm afraid," she told me. "I know it's an inconvenience, but it's part of the process."

"I understand," I told her. "I don't know who's still at the inn; do you want me to tell whoever's there to stay put till you get there?"

"That would be great," she said.

"I'll whip up some scones while I'm there," I said.

"There's no need for that."

"I'm working on a recipe for a competition anyway," I said. "It's no trouble."

"That would be wonderful, then," she said. "We'll be down in a bit. John, do you mind staying?" she asked my handsome husband. She was an attractive woman in her forties, with a physique that suggested long hours in the gym and a very limited acquaintance with coffee cake. "We're a bit short-handed, and we may need your help figuring out who's who at the co-op."

"Happy to," he said.

"I'll see you soon," I told him, planting a big kiss on my husband before heading back down to the inn.

7

*B*iscuit and Smudge were busy chasing a fake mouse around the kitchen floor and I'd just finished toasting a pan of walnuts when John came back into the kitchen, smelling like sea air and the rain that had started coming down a few minutes earlier.

"I called Tom and told him to call off the hunt; he was relieved she was found on land."

"That doesn't mean a lobsterman isn't responsible," John said with a grimace.

"I know, but at least it broadens the possibilities, I guess. I still can't believe she's dead; she was so young! And she'd hardly gotten to the island."

"I know." John took off his windbreaker and poured himself a cup of coffee, then slumped into a kitchen chair. Smudge immediately hopped into his lap, put her paws on his chest, and touched her nose to his. John smiled and scratched the top of her head.

"Did they get things squared away before the weather kicked in?" I asked.

"Enough," he said. "Something smells good. What are you making?"

"Maple walnut scones," I said as I cut butter into a bowl of dry ingredients. "I'm trying to find a winner for the scone competition in the Portland paper. I figure the publicity will help."

"Bookings are still down, then?"

"They are," I said. "I might see if I can set up some kind of art retreat with Gwen, where people stay here for the week and take classes at the Guild."

"That sounds like a great idea. We should probably put out a newsletter soon, too."

"I was thinking we might run some specials, or maybe put together a getaway weekend package." I added the liquid ingredients to the crumbly mixture in the bowl. "With everything that's going on, though, I don't know when I'm going to do it. I told Catherine I'd join her at her pottery class this afternoon."

"I didn't know you were interested in pottery."

"I'm not. Well, I am, but I'd rather learn to make mugs and bowls than the bulbous sea creatures that seem to be his specialty. I didn't want her going there alone," I said. "Just in case."

John cocked an eyebrow. "You think Chad's a murderer?"

"Someone is," I said. "He's the only person I know who knew Chelsea."

He sighed. "As much as I hate to think it, I'm guessing it may be someone in the lobstering community. Tempers have been running hot lately, and you know lobstermen are an independent bunch. They don't like people nosing in."

"If that's the case, though, I'm betting someone has something to hide. No one's going to kill an observer just on principle."

"Illegal fishing?" he asked as I added the walnuts to the scone dough.

"On a grand scale, maybe. Either that, or something else criminal is going on. At least that's what Sally thinks, and I tend to agree with her."

"Sally? The detective?" I asked, trying to quell the little bubble of jealousy that floated up at the mention of the detective's first name. The Catherine-Murray-Sarah situation must be getting to me. I gave myself a little shake and put on a smile, dismissing my reaction. "Like what?"

"Yes, Sally Freedman," he confirmed. "As for the criminal issue, I don't know," he continued. "We've had drug-running before, but I hate to think that any of the islanders might be involved with that."

I shrugged. "I just hope they find out before something else happens."

"So much for the idyllic island life," John said with a grimace.

"It does have its perks, though," I said as I turned the dough out onto a board. "I'd rather be working here than a cubicle somewhere."

"That's true," he said, coming up behind me and putting his arms around my waist. He gave me a kiss on the back of the neck. "And the lunch service is fabulous. Plus, I love my coworkers."

"Me too," I said, leaning back into him. "The drop in bookings is just a temporary thing, right?"

"It is," he said. "There are ups and downs. We just have to remind our former guests that we're here and reach out to some new ones, and we'll be turning away bookings."

"I hope you're right," I told him.

"We'll make it work, sweetheart," he said. "One way or the other. I promise."

I closed my eyes for a moment, thankful to have met such a wonderful, supportive man. "I'm glad you're in my life," I told him.

Catherine walked into the kitchen, her arms filled with dirty towels. "Sorry to interrupt," she said as John kissed me on top of the head and stepped away.

"You're not interrupting," I told her. "Thanks for taking care of the rooms."

"It's no trouble," she said. "I did leave the Rose Room alone until the police have a chance to look at it."

"Thanks. Are any of the other guests in their rooms?" I asked. "I know the investigators are going to want to talk with them."

She shook her head. "Everyone's out for the day. I imagine the artists are at the Guild. There was a 'Do Not Disturb' sign on the couple's room—Noelle and Bruce, right?—so I don't know if they're here. I think that Sarah woman was headed to the mainland today." She frowned. "Her room is kind of a mess. And she reads romance novels."

"Lots of people read romance novels," I pointed out.

Catherine sniffed. "You'd think she'd at least clean the toothpaste out of the sink. I'm telling you, it was a mess in there. And she wears some perfume that smells like the back of my grandmother's attic. Plus, she spends a fortune on beauty products."

John and I exchanged glances.

"Did you notice anything out of the ordinary in any of the other rooms?" I asked.

"Not really," she said. "Although Chad's room is as bad as Sarah's. I guess they're used to other people picking up after them." Her brow wrinkled. "There was a woman's barrette in Chad's room, though, next to the bed. I put it on the night-stand. Maybe it belongs to the poor young woman?"

"That's interesting," I said. "I don't remember Chelsea wearing a barrette, though."

"Maybe one of the other artists visited him in his room," John suggested. "He seemed interested in Emma."

"From what I saw, it wasn't superreciprocal, but I guess we'll see what we can find out today at the Guild," I said.

"You're coming with me still, right?" Catherine asked.

"If it's okay with you," I said.

"Of course!" she said. "Maybe we can make mugs for the inn!"

From what I'd seen of Chad's work, I was guessing mugs weren't on the agenda, but I just smiled. "Here's hoping!"

DETECTIVE FREEDMAN CAME in a few minutes later, asking if I knew where she could find my guests. I drew a rough map for her, giving her directions to the Art Guild to find the artist guests and to Cliffside to track down Sarah.

"Thanks," she said. "I haven't really asked you any questions yet. What made you and John go looking on the path for Chelsea Sanchez?"

"Like I said, Tom called me at around nine thirty to let me know she hadn't turned up at the dock; she was supposed to meet Mac at nine. I was going to drive her over to the dock, but she decided to walk over on the early side."

"Why did she decide to walk?"

"Like I said, she had a bit of an exchange with one of our other guests, one of the artists at the Guild. I think she was a bit upset."

"His name is Chad, right?" she asked.

"Yes. Chad Berman. They knew each other; she called him a trust-fund baby. He didn't take to it too well."

"Interesting," she said, jotting down notes. "And I can find him at the Art Guild?"

"Presumably," I replied. "He's a potter."

"Did she know anyone else in the dining room?" the detective asked.

"Not that I could tell," I said. My thoughts touched on Bruce and Noelle, who had quickly made themselves scarce, but they hadn't interacted with Chelsea at all. "She did seem a bit... startled, or almost upset, at one point, though."

"Upset?"

"Yes," I said. "I think it may have been her conversation with Chad. Apparently they knew each other in college."

"Any idea what it was about?"

"Other than the trust-fund baby thing, I don't know."

"I'LL BE sure to talk to him. Who else was in the dining room at the time?" the detective asked.

"Just about everyone. Chad, of course. And Thuy, Emma, Sarah, Bruce and Noelle..." I ticked off the guests' names on my fingers. "Everyone came down early this morning."

"And you don't know if there was anything else she might be reacting to? That startled her?"

"No," I said, shaking my head. "I wish I did. I'm sorry."

"And she didn't interact with anyone else while she was here? Did you notice any visitors to the inn, other than the guests?"

I shook my head. "I'll ask Catherine and John, but none that I saw."

"Oh, don't worry about John. I'll talk with him in a bit. But if you could ask Catherine, that would be helpful."

Again, I felt that twinge of jealousy, but I just smiled. "I'll ask her. Let me know if there's anything else we can do to help."

"Thanks, Natalie," she said with a bright smile. "You and John have been great. I saw some of his sculptures on the mainland recently, by the way... he really is talented!"

"He is," I said.

"At any rate, duty calls," she said. "And do you have a key to Chelsea's room? Has anyone been in there?"

"I let myself in to look for her, but I didn't touch anything," I said, digging in my pocket and producing a key. "It's on the first floor, near the end of the hall; it's called the Rose Room."

"Thanks," she said. "Talk to you soon, I'm sure," she said as she strode toward the swinging door to the rest of the inn, leaving me alone and unsettled in my kitchen.

THE PHONE at the inn rang constantly that afternoon: not with bookings, unfortunately, but with curious islanders—and, even worse, Gertrude Pickens of the *Daily Mail*, who was always sniffing around for a story.

Her syrupy voice made me want to hang up the moment I heard it. "Natalie! I'm so glad I caught you."

"I'm actually on my way out..."

"I'll only be a moment. I heard one of your guests died," she said. "The observer who was supposed to be on Mac Penney's boat. I understand there's been a lot of bad blood on Cranberry Island recently."

"I don't know about that," I said. "I pretty much stick to inn business."

"Did you meet the young woman? Chelsea Sanchez, right? You must have, because she was staying at your inn."

"I don't think I'm supposed to talk about it."

"So the police are investigating," she said in an excited tone. I bit my lip. "My sources tell me someone hit her over the head. Can you confirm that?"

Gertrude's sources were pretty darned good, it seemed. I wondered if she had an in at the police station; none of the islanders who had called knew as much as she did, or if they did, they hadn't mentioned it. "Gertrude, I'm on my way out the door. I'm sorry, but I can't help you."

"She didn't die at the inn, though, did she?"

"No," I confirmed. The last thing I needed was an article claiming that a guest had died here. Bookings were bad enough as it was.

"So, no statement you'd like to give?"

I took a deep breath. "Not at the moment, no," I said. "Let me think about it."

"Don't think too long," she said. "Deadline's at five."

"Got it," I said, cursing under my breath as I hung up. I had a bad feeling about this article Gertrude was working on. Should I make a statement? Or would that just make things worse? I had no idea. But I did know I had to head over to the Art Guild for the pottery class with Chad Berman and my mother-in-law. I knocked on Catherine's door, but there was no answer—she must have left early— so I got on my blue bike and headed up the drive.

THE RAIN HAD PASSED, leaving the island feeling fresh and clean; droplets still clung to the white blueberry blossoms, and the cool, moist air brought out the piney scent of balsam. I rolled up to the Art Guild a few minutes early, hoping to catch Gwen before the class started. As I parked my bike against one of the blooming apple trees, I heard the sound of hammering from one of the outbuildings. The doors were open to let in the cool spring air; I walked over to find my niece, in goggles, assembling a simple wood frame for one of her pieces inside.

She looked up as I knocked on the door. "Hey," she said, putting down the hammer. "Any more news about poor Chelsea?"

"Not yet," I said, raising an eyebrow. "No one keeping you company?"

"Thuy just stepped out for a snack," she said, tilting her head toward the other worktable, where an intricate tree was taking shape from a stack of thin trunk slices. "She said she'd only be a minute." She lowered her voice. "Do you really think it might be Chad?"

"I don't know who it is," I told her. "But he's the only person I really saw her interact with, and it didn't go well, so I'm erring on the side of caution. What do you know about him?"

"Well, his family put up half the money to get the Guild going," she said. "They live over in Northeast Harbor. He got an MFA degree from Middlesex about five years ago and has been doing art ever since, but I don't know how much he actually sells," she said diplomatically. "He says he's more interested in art for art's sake than art for commerce."

"Ah," I said. "How does he get along with the other folks here?"

"He lets them know where the money's coming from, that's for sure. But I think he's jealous, frankly. Of Thuy in particular; her work sells for a lot."

"I'm not surprised," I said, admiring her work in progress.

"I think Chad thinks his should be selling for at least as

much. He's talking about doing a bigger project, maybe a clay sculpture, but he'd need a bigger kiln.... He's lobbying his parents for one now."

"Must be nice to have backers you're related to," I said. "When did he get here this morning?"

"Around nine thirty," she said.

"Was he with anyone? Maybe Emma?"

She shook her head. "She got here about half an hour earlier. He was the last one here, actually."

"Anything else you can think of?"

"Wow," Gwen said, raising her dark eyebrows. "You really are going after him."

"No... not yet, anyway. I'm just gathering information. If you're going to be spending all day around him, I'd like to be sure he's not homicidal." As I spoke, Thuy walked into the workshop, eating a banana.

"Who's homicidal?" she asked, blinking. She wore a faded apron over jeans and a plaid shirt, and there was sawdust in her black hair.

"Aunt Nat's just trying to figure out what happened to Chelsea," Gwen informed her.

Thuy shook her head. "That's so sad... I still can't believe it!" She was a few years older than Gwen, maybe in her early- to mid-thirties, but with the presence and self-confidence of a woman much older. Even though John was several years older, I knew he'd learned a lot from her since she arrived on the island a few weeks earlier. "Emma told me she fell on the path by the cliffs and hit her head." Thuy looked at me. "Is that not what happened?"

"Where did Emma hear that?" I asked.

Thuy shrugged. "You'd have to ask her. I would rather think it was an accident. I'd heard there was some friction down at the co-op, but homicide?"

"I shouldn't have said that," I admitted. "I really don't have a lot of information about what's going on."

"At least not for now," Gwen said, giving me a sidelong look. "Between you and Charlene, it's hard to get away with anything on this island."

"Have you been trying?" I asked.

"I know better," she said, and glanced at her watch. "Pottery class starts in five minutes. Where's Catherine?"

"I should probably find out," I said, and eyed both women. "Be careful, both of you. And stick together."

It wasn't until I was ten steps away from the workshop that I realized I really didn't know much about Thuy Nguyen, and that perhaps that wasn't the best advice.

8

*C*atherine and I comprised fully half of Chad's class, which was held in a small room with two large tables. My mother-in-law's eyes were red, and when I asked where she'd been, she told me she'd taken a walk to clear her mind. I slid into a chair next to her and glanced around the room. The other two participants included my friend, Emmeline Hoyle, who was a crack knitter, and a young woman I didn't recognize. They occupied the other table.

Although it was a few minutes after three, there was no sign of Chad.

"Do you think we'll get to do mugs?" Emmeline asked. "I'm hoping to make a set for my niece for Christmas."

"I was hoping to do some for the inn!" Catherine added. "Maybe we can ask to learn mugs."

"I doubt he'll teach us that," the young woman said. She had short, black hair and wore an artfully distressed black dress and leggings. "He's not in to production pottery; he prefers one-of-a-kind pieces. He told me we're going to work on creating organic forms."

"Organic forms?" Emmeline asked. "Like rocks?"

"Whatever you like," she replied. "Oh, look. Here he is!" She adjusted the neckline of her dress and sat up straight as Chad swaggered into the room.

"Good afternoon, everyone!" he said.

"Hi, Chad," the young woman simpered. Catherine glanced at me and rolled her eyes.

"Hi, Quartz," he replied.

Catherine cocked a tweezed eyebrow.

"Good to see you. As you know, we're going to be experimenting with clay this session. Have any of you taken a pottery class before?"

Quartz's hand shot up in the air, her bangles clinking as they slid down to her elbow. Emmeline raised a tentative hand.

"I know you, of course," Chad said, giving Quartz a smug smile before glancing at Emmeline. "So, about half of you. If you've had one before, I'm sure you were expecting to use a wheel today, maybe do a basic bowl. But we're going to do things a little bit differently here."

"What do you mean, differently?" Catherine asked.

"We're going to explore the clay," he said, grabbing a lump of wet clay from a plastic bin at the front of the room and holding it in his hands. "You have to feel the clay," he said. "Let it tell you what it wants to be." As we watched, he massaged the clay in both hands. Had one of those hands held the rock that ended Chelsea's life? I wondered. If he had murdered her that morning, it didn't seem to be troubling his conscience. I glanced at Quartz, who had a look on her pale face that suggested she wished she could be that lump of clay. I looked away quickly.

"I'll let you try it yourselves," he said, handing his deformed lump to Quartz, who cradled it in her hands as if he had gifted her a ruby, then fishing out three more lumps and distributing them to the rest of us. "Now," he said. "Just play with it. Feel it. I'll put on some music to help you get into the mood."

As we all picked up the cold clay, he fumbled with his iPhone. A moment later, a tinny recording of some rhythmic drumming music filled the small room. "Close your eyes," he exhorted us. "Become one with the clay."

I didn't close my eyes. It was too much fun watching Catherine and Emmeline trying to figure out what to do with these instructions. While Quartz had closed her eyes and was swaying back as forth as she massaged her clay, both Emmeline and Catherine sat stick-straight. Emmeline hadn't closed her eyes either, but had started kneading her lump as if it were bread dough. Catherine, on the other hand, gave it a tentative poke with her finger, then spent the next ten seconds extracting clay from beneath her fingernail.

"You're not feeling the clay," Chad chided me.

"Oh," I said. "Sorry." I took the cold clay and squeezed it, then squeezed it again. It was kind of satisfying, but the clay didn't seem to have any ideas about what it wanted to be.

This went on for what must have been at least fifteen minutes, although it felt longer. By the time Chad turned off the music, Quartz was swaying back and forth in a quasi-meditative state, Emmeline had progressed from kneading to rolling out bits of clay that reminded me of breadsticks, and Catherine was patting her ball of clay as if it were a favorite pet.

"Now that we've gotten acquainted with our clay," Chad said, "let's try forming it. Can you make a snake?"

Emmeline had already made several snakes, but she gamely began attaching them to each other to make a long one. I rolled my clay beneath my hands, feeling foolish, while Catherine raised her hand.

"Yes?" he asked.

"Are we going to be using a wheel anytime soon?"

"Eventually, yes," he said.

"Will you teach us to make mugs?" she asked.

He let out a contemptuous-sounding noise. "This is an art class, not a craft class. We're making art."

"Mugs aren't art?" Catherine challenged him.

"Mugs are utilitarian items," he said. "They are not expressions of the artist's vision. Now," he said, dismissing the question, "follow your instincts and create a form. Let the image bubble up in your head, and let your hands create it in the clay." He returned to his iPhone and turned on another tinny tune. Catherine and Emmeline looked at each other. I got the distinct impression that the class wasn't exactly what they had expected.

BY THE TIME the first session was over, Quartz had made a lumpish thing with tentacles and spikes she called a "jella-nenomefish," and both Emmeline and Catherine had evidently had clay that wanted to be made into rudimentary mugs. "So, we'll start with the wheel next time?" Catherine asked as we put our creations—mine looked kind of like a mutant sea slug—onto a shelf.

"We'll see," he said vaguely.

Quartz and I lingered after class, but for very different reasons. "Are we still on for dinner in Northeast Harbor tonight?" Quartz asked.

"It'll have to be early," he said. "The last mail boat leaves the mainland at around six."

"You could always stay the night," she said, then glanced at me. "On the couch, of course."

"I'll see how the work goes," he said, dismissing her. "I'm trying to get ready for that gallery show, and the sponges aren't looking quite right. Can I text you this afternoon?"

"Sure," she said with a shrug that didn't conceal her hurt feelings. Something sparkled in her dark hair as she moved; it was a small butterfly barrette covered in dark crystals. "Thanks for the class; it was great. I really felt one with the clay."

Chad's face broke into a smile. "I'm glad you got it," he said, and his eyes slid to me. "Not everyone does."

She smiled back, obviously buoyed by his response. "Thanks. I'm going to go down to the shore for inspiration. Text me later!"

"Uh-huh," he said, then turned to me. "Can I help you?"

"Thanks for the class," I said. "I never thought about clay that way before."

"It's a different approach, but I think it really opens up the creative pathways," he said.

"It was really interesting. Oh—by the way—how did you know Chelsea Sanchez?"

His sunny face darkened. "I heard what happened to her this morning. Tragic."

"Who told you?"

"Everyone was buzzing about it," he replied, and busied himself making sure the clay tub was sealed. "The police came and talked with us briefly, too. I don't remember who told me."

"How did you meet her?"

"We were at school together," he told me. "It was a long time ago. We took a few classes together. I hadn't seen her since."

"It didn't look like you were particularly good friends," I said.

"She liked to razz me," he said. "We were okay, though. Anyway, I've got to run... big gallery show coming up. Glad you enjoyed the class."

"Thanks for teaching it. See you later, then." He was still fiddling with the clay bin when I walked out of the studio; I got the impression Chelsea wasn't a topic he wanted to linger on.

Why? I wondered.

And I thought of the barrette I saw next to Chad's bed. Had Quartz spent the night in his room? And if so, what, if anything, did that have to do with Chelsea Sanchez?

I walked down the hallway away from the studio. I hadn't gotten to the door before I heard Chad's voice. "Yeah, it's me," he said. "Remember that chick from school? The one who constantly gave me a hard time, and wrote in the school paper about my parents paying for me to get in, and started that investigation?" I could hear the faint voice of someone on the other end of the phone, then, "Well, someone capped her this morning." More talking from the other end of the line. "Yeah. Can you believe she turned up on the island? Some kind of fisheries' observer or some- thing, going out on lobster boats; the art thing didn't pan out for her, I guess. Anyway, she's staying at the same inn as me... or she was. She saw me at breakfast this morning and gave me a hard time about being a 'trust-fund baby' again, and then she died like a half hour later. I know it's bad to say, but it kind of serves her right." He paused, and I could hear the person on the other end talking. "No, I don't know how or where. But the police came and talked to me, and it's freaking me out." Another pause. "Dude, of course it wasn't me!" More talking on the other end, agitated this time. "I was just talking smack. You know that. At any rate, I just wanted to give you a heads-up, in case anyone tries to get in touch with you." The other person talked for a bit, then Chad responded. "Yeah. Not a lot of action here; there's a chick named Quartz, but she's just taking the class because she's into me. Then there are two old biddies and the chunky, middle-aged woman who runs the inn."

Two old biddies and a chunky, middle-aged woman? I resisted the urge to march back down the hall and smack him myself. I could only imagine what Catherine would think of that description of her and Emmeline. As I controlled my own murderous impulses, Chad continued. "I probably should have done the New York thing instead, but this is what my parents were willing to do, so, you know. At least Quartz is hot; she stayed over the other night."

Well, that answered the barrette question.

"Anyway, I've got to run; I've got work to do. Let me know if you hear anything, okay?"

I didn't wait to hear any more, and let myself quietly out the door. I could see why Chelsea wasn't Chad's biggest fan. I certainly wasn't, either.

And now I was curious about what "investigation" Chelsea had instigated... and whether anything had come of it.

9

*C*atherine had already started back to the inn to get ready for her date with Murray, so after checking in on Thuy and Gwen and extracting a promise that Adam would escort my niece home, I headed over to the store to check in with Charlene.

"You didn't call me!" she said when I walked in the door. Eli was ensconced on one of the squashy sofas in the front of the store, a scone in one hand and a mug of tea in the other, but otherwise the store was surprisingly empty.

"Sorry," I said. "It's been a crazy day." I turned to Eli. "How's Claudette?"

"Still waiting for results," he said dolefully. "She sleeps all the time these days; it's not like her. I'm hoping it's just a touch of depression."

"I hope so, too," I said. "The waiting's got to be hard."

"The hardest," he replied, looking worn. "You hear what happened to the fleet?"

"I did," I said. "Any luck finding the missing boats yet?"

"We've only found some of them," Charlene said. "Two were grounded, three were caught up in fishing lines out between here and MDI, and three more are still missing... including Adam's boat. And Mac's."

"That's terrible!" I said. "Who do you think did it?"

She shrugged. "Nobody knows."

"Has Tom called the Marine Patrol?"

"Not yet," Charlene said. "Not too much damage so far, and no one on the island wants outsiders involved, particularly with everything that's been going on lately."

"That's what he told me." I sighed. "So no one was out to sea this morning." Which meant just about anyone on the island could have done in Chelsea.

"I saw the police launch and heard from Tom that you had some excitement out by the inn, too," Charlene said.

"We did," I confirmed. "Chelsea disappeared after breakfast. We found her on the cliff path."

"I heard it wasn't an accident," she said in a soft voice. "The whole island is buzzing; you just missed a whole contingent of lobstermen."

"I'll wait to hear the official report," I said, "but Gertrude Pickens called me and wanted a statement for the paper. I want to know what happened to poor Chelsea, but I'm also worried about what's going to happen to the inn if she blasts something untrue." I sighed. "Besides, the last thing I need is another murder connected with the inn."

"So you do think it's murder?"

"I don't know, but circumstances were a bit... well, weird." I grimaced. "Should I give her a statement or say nothing?"

Charlene bit her frosted lip. "When does she need it by?"

"Five," I said.

Charlene glanced up at the clock. "You've got forty minutes to figure it out. I think you should say something so she doesn't put words in your mouth."

"Maybe something along the lines of 'We are saddened

by this tragedy, and our hearts and prayers are with Chelsea's family?'" I suggested.

"That sounds perfect," she said. "Why don't you call and tell her now?"

"I think I will," I said, and pulled out my cell phone. Gertrude didn't answer; I left her a message, thankful to be able to cross that off my mental list.

"Tom told me he thinks someone in the co-op might be involved in what happened," Charlene told me when I put the phone back in my pocket.

"Why does he think that?"

"Chelsea's arrival wasn't popular," she said. "Mac wasn't exactly a fan, obviously. And there's been talk about Adam, too."

"Gwen's Adam? What about him?"

"He's had a good run lately," she said. "There's some talk that he's fishing hidden traps. I heard Earl suggesting that maybe Adam did Chelsea in so she couldn't find out what he was up to."

"That makes no sense at all," I said. "She wasn't even scheduled to be on his boat."

"The word on the street is that she was an undercover officer," Charlene said. "You know tempers have been hot here lately."

"I do," I acknowledged. "Which is why Eli's got the *Lucky Lady* in his workshop. I just can't imagine that someone would kill an innocent young woman over potential fishing infractions."

"I don't know," Charlene said. "For a lot of the folks here, lobstering is the only job they've got training for. The penalties for illegal fishing are pretty steep: Having your license suspended for a few years—or permanently—could mean total ruin for a lobsterman."

"Ayuh," Eli agreed from the couch. "I'm not sayin' it was anyone from the co-op, but there's a lot ridin' on those licenses."

"Adam told me Mac wasn't going to let her on his boat," Charlene said. "Do you think maybe Mac decided to get rid of her before she got to the dock?"

"It's a thought," I said. "I hate to think of anyone on the island being responsible for what happened to Chelsea."

Charlene quirked up a penciled eyebrow. "Do you have any other ideas?"

"I don't know that much about her, unfortunately," I said. "But Chad Berman is certainly on my list."

"He's one of the artists, right?"

"Yeah. There was some bad blood between them. Apparently, she accused him of buying his way into college when they were in school; got an article in the school paper about it and started an investigation."

"That's certainly bad blood," she said. "But why kill her now? I mean, college is in the rearview mirror for both of them, presumably."

"I don't know," I said. "It's worth asking about, though."

"Anyone else?" she asked.

"No," I said.

"Except Adam," Eli offered from the couch.

"Still? But he's such a good guy!" I protested."

"He's not from the island," Eli said. "A few people still got a grudge that he got his license. And that Ivy League degree of his don't help."

My niece's husband had earned a degree from Princeton before chucking it overboard—literally—and starting a new career as a lobsterman here on the island. Normally, I didn't hear much negative talk about him, and he seemed like an accepted member of the lobstering community, but it seemed with tensions so high lately, some of that goodwill had evaporated.

"Anyone else saying that?" I asked.

"Not that I've heard yet," he said, "but she just turned up this morning. There's a good chance that isn't the last we've heard of it."

"I hope he's got a good alibi," I said.

"He wasn't on the *Carpe Diem* this morning, I know that," he said.

"How about Mac? Was he out before nine?"

Eli shook his head. "Neither one of 'em showed up to the co-op before nine, from what I hear."

Surely Adam had been at home with Gwen, I told myself, but I felt uneasy. "Anyone else from the co-op making noise about an observer coming to the island?" I asked.

"Oh, there's griping, of course, but Mac's the main one. Well, him and Earl," he said.

"What did Earl say?"

"Just that things were better before all this regulatory stuff, and it's our taxes paying for invasion of privacy. He's a pretty strong libertarian, you know."

"Not surprising," Charlene added. "Lobstermen are an independent bunch."

She'd barely finished speaking when the bell above the door rang, and Mac Penney strode in, wearing a wild beard, a stained plaid shirt, and overalls tucked into black rubber boots.

"Howdy there, Mac," Eli said, tipping an imaginary cap.

Mac grunted. "Got any PBR in stock?" he asked Charlene.

She pointed to the cooler. "Just refilled it last night," she said. "Did you hear the news?"

He shot her a piercing look from bloodshot eyes. "About that investigator? Ayuh." He opened the cooler door and pulled out a case of Pabst Blue Ribbon. "Guess that's what happens when you stick your nose in where it's not wanted," he said.

"She wasn't an investigator," I pointed out.

"Observer, investigator... same difference. Tryin' to catch me out on the littlest thing. I'm an honest man. Always have been."

Charlene and I exchanged looks; I had a feeling she had some inside information on that.

"Know anything about what happened to her?" Charlene asked.

"Only what everyone else knows," he said. "Took a tumble and got brained on the cliff walk. Probably wearing city shoes."

"She was wearing boots, actually," I said. Bean boots, in fact; I'd noticed as I waited by her side that morning.

"Well, not used to rocky terrain, then," he said, putting the case of beer on the counter alongside a can of Sour Cream & Onion Pringles and fishing a wad of bills out of his overalls. "How much?"

"Twenty dollars and forty-two cents," Charlene informed him after she rang up his purchases.

He forked over a twenty and a one, and she counted out his change.

"Know anyone else who wasn't happy about her coming to the island?" I asked Mac.

His blue eyes swung to me. "Not offhand," he said, sizing me up. "Why?"

"Just curious," I said. "I don't like it when bad things happen to my guests."

"So, you think someone did away with her, is that it?"

I shrugged. "I don't know what happened. I'm just curious about it, is all."

"Well," he said, holding my gaze, "if I were you, I'd mind my own business. Curiosity killed the cat, as they say."

There was a menace in his gruff voice that made me swallow hard.

"You sound like you're threatening her," Charlene said coolly.

Mac shrugged and hefted the case of beer under one arm and grabbed the potato chips with the other. "I'm just stating the obvious," he said. "Good afternoon," he said formally to all of us, then ambled out of the store, leaving the smell of cigarette smoke, old beer, and herring in his wake.

10

"*Well*," Charlene said when the door swung closed. "I'd put him on the top of your suspect list, for sure." She turned to me. "Don't take it too personally, though. He's always had a thing against anyone who wasn't born on the island."

"He seemed more worried about me poking into his business," I said thoughtfully. "And usually, people who are worried about that have something to hide."

"I can't say you're wrong," Eli said from the couch. "But go easy with that one. He's got a temper."

"I know," I said, remembering what had happened to the *Lucky Lady*. "Speaking of a temper, any more exchanges between Mac and Earl?"

"Not that I've heard," Eli said, "but I wouldn't call it resolved."

Charlene was still staring at the door. "Do you think he's taking that out on his boat?" she asked.

"Likely," Eli said.

She sighed. "I hate to say it, but I probably need to give Tom a heads-up. And I hope Josie's driving today."

"I don't know how she puts up with him," I said.

"She's a distant cousin," Charlene said. "I think he's nicer to her than he is to the average person."

"That's not saying much," I pointed out.

"True," said Eli with the first grin I'd seen.

"How are you holding up?"

"On pins and needles waiting for results."

"I hope there's nothing to it," I said.

"Oh, believe me, so do we," he said, taking another swig of his tea and getting up. "I'd better get back to work on the *Lucky Lady*," he said.

"Let us know when you hear anything, okay?" I asked.

"Of course," he said. I couldn't help noticing that his shoulders slumped as he headed toward the door of the store.

I MADE a quick dinner of cod a la meunière that night—a simple fish dish sautéed in brown butter sauce, served with asparagus, roasted potatoes, and a blueberry crumble for dessert. John had spent most of the day with Thuy, and now that the police had headed back to the mainland, he was in his workshop catching up on what he'd planned to do earlier. I missed his presence in the kitchen as I arranged asparagus on the guests' plates. If he'd found out anything else about the case, he hadn't told me; I knew the police had been to the Art Guild to talk with the artists, and I'd seen them talking with Bruce and Noelle in the parlor earlier, but I didn't know what else they'd managed to turn up that day. I hoped it was an accident, but unfortunately, I suspected the odds were slim.

Sarah was the only guest not in attendance tonight, as

she was off on the mainland for dinner; presumably, she was taking a water taxi back or had a ride from someone with a boat, because the last mail boat had long since gone. Catherine had been picked up by Murray in his Jaguar before dinner service began, after debating outfits for an hour, looking more excited and almost nervous than I'd seen her even at the beginning of their courtship. I hoped things were going better between them, but I still had a niggling feeling.

It was a fairly full house, but the dining room was almost eerily silent. .

The two lovebirds were remarkably restrained; in fact, Bruce spent most of dinner checking his phone, and the PDAs had declined to an occasional sympathetic pat on the hand from Noelle, who also looked pained. "Can I get you some blueberry crumble?" I asked as I cleared their plates.

"Sure," Noelle said in a lackluster tone of voice. There was a crease between her dark eyebrows I hadn't seen the day before.

"Me too," Bruce said. Both were in their forties, and obviously worked to stay in shape. I wondered how long they'd been seeing each other—and why the change in mood.

"I'll bring two in a moment," I assured them, and gathered their dinner plates; half the cod was still on Noelle's plate, and Bruce's was barely touched. Bad news from home? I wondered as I took the plates into the kitchen. At least Biscuit and Smudge would be happy, I thought as I spooned the leftover fish into their bowls. It was almost gone by the time I'd dished out the crumble.

I ferried dessert out to the lovebirds and checked on the artists' table. Chad was sitting next to Emma again, and I got the impression—again—that Chad was more interested in her than the other way around. He was asking about how helpful her MFA had been, and getting one-word answers. Apparently, dinner with Quartz had been scotched, poor thing... but something told me she wouldn't give up that easily. Thuy sat across from them, doodling in a notebook and lost in thought... altogether not the most congenial group.

"Blueberry crumble?" I asked the table, and got three yeses. The plates were mostly clean... maybe the starving artist bit was a real thing, I thought as I stacked them up. There was hardly a bite left.

I glanced at the table where Chelsea had briefly sat that morning, and felt a pang. Who had cut her young life short? Was it an islander?

Or, I thought as I headed back to the kitchen again, was it one of my guests?

I had just delivered three more plates of crumble when the phone rang. I hurried back into the kitchen; it was Eli.

"What's up?" I asked.

"Don't say anything to anyone... but will you come down here?"

"Is Claudette okay?"

"Oh, yes... it's nothing to do with that," he said. "But I just found something on the *Lucky Lady*, and I want to see what you think."

I glanced up at the clock. "I've got some cleanup to do here, but I'll be down in an hour, okay?"

"That'll work," he said. I hung up the phone a moment later, wondering what Eli had found... and why he wanted to show me.

IT WAS dark by the time I got to Claudette and Eli's. The

wind had kicked up, coming in restless gusts that blew hair up into my face as I walked, and clouds were scudding over the star-studded sky as if they were racing somewhere. I found myself wishing I'd put on a sweater as I stepped onto the porch, hugging myself. Eli answered the door even before I knocked. "I don't want to wake up Claudie," he explained in a hushed voice. "She went to bed early."

"Got it," I said. "What did you find?"

"I'll show you," he said, putting on his boots. "Follow me."

A sharp gust tugged at my windbreaker as I followed my friend out to his workshop, wondering what he'd found on the *Lucky Lady*. Drugs? Incriminating evidence? I just didn't know.

Eli opened the big garage door to his workshop and flipped on the lights, making the darkness outside more impenetrable. "Climb on board," he said, climbing the short ladder to the boat with an agility that belied his age. I followed, rather less gracefully, and a moment later, was standing next to him on deck of the *Lucky Lady*. It was weird to be on a lobster boat in a barn.

"I found it back here," he said, leading me to the back of the boat. "I took off this washboard, see," he said, removing a panel on the back of the boat to expose a plastic tub with a pump in it.

"What is it?" I asked.

"It's a holding tank," he said. "I noticed the tube down below the boat," he said. "It's the water intake; there's another one on the other side."

"So it's a hidden holding tank," I said. "What's he been keeping in it?"

"Illegal lobsters is my guess," he said. "I'm surprised he let me have his boat; he had to guess I might find it."

"Although the damage is in the front," I said. "He probably figured you'd never look elsewhere."

"Then he doesn't know me very well," Eli said. "If he is storing illegal lobsters—shorts or berried lobsters—he knows the co-op would never buy them."

"Berried lobsters... that's females with eggs, right?"

"Right," he confirmed.

"So what's he doing with them?" I asked.

"Selling them to someone, I'm guessing," he answered. "Someone willing to take the risk."

"I heard a rumor about a few lobster pounds on the mainland," I said. "Selling to tourists who can't tell the difference."

"Could be it," he said. "Maybe there was something to that poor young woman being here undercover. Looks like some shady business going on."

"Do you think Earl might have killed her to keep her from discovering that?"

"You can lose a license for years over something like this," he said. "These folks don't know how to do anything but this. If they can't fish..." He made a cutting gesture over his throat.

"Stakes are pretty high, then," I said. "So why do it?"

"Money," Eli said with a sigh. "It always seems to be about money."

Unfortunately, it often did. "But why would Earl risk losing his license over it?"

"Must have needed cash bad. His daughter's at the University of Maine, and he was grousing about the cost the other day."

"Maybe tuition payments put the squeeze on him?"

"Maybe."

I looked at the empty compartment. "What do we do about it?"

He shrugged. "There aren't any lobsters in there now. Nothing illegal to report."

"Are you going to say anything to him about it?"

"I don't know," he told me. "I don't know what to do."

"I don't know either," I replied. "Should we tell the fisheries people?"

"I thought about that," he told me. "I don't like cheating. And I don't like people messing with the resource. But Earl is one of ours. If he gets his license suspended, how is he going to keep on?"

"It's a tough call," I agreed. "I also wonder how many other lobstermen have these secret compartments."

"I don't know," he said. "I never built one, I'll tell you that. I don't get involved in shady stuff like that."

I wasn't surprised. "Ironic that Mac thought Earl snitched on him, isn't it?"

"Ayuh," Eli said as he put the washboard back on. "I'll sleep on it."

"Thanks for letting me know," I said as he finished putting it back on. The two of us walked to the barn door, and he switched off the light. "How's Claudette doing?" I asked in a quiet voice.

"I'm worried," he said. "If I lose her..."

I reached out and touched his shoulder. Together, we walked to the house in a silence punctuated only by the wind whipping past the roof; it was getting chilly, and it smelled like rain. When we got to the porch, I said, "We're all here for you, you know."

"I know," he said. "Thank you."

"Of course," I replied.

"Don't say anything about what I showed you, okay? Not even to John," Eli cautioned me.

I didn't like it, but I agreed. At least for now.

"Get some sleep," I told him. "I'll stop by tomorrow with some food. And I might sneak a few scones in, too."

"Thank you, Nat," Eli said, his face crinkling into a weary smile. "I'm glad you came to Cranberry Island."

"Me too," I said, giving him a hug before turning back to the inn.

THE RAIN STARTED as I hit the top of the driveway, coming down in sheets that cut through my light windbreaker and soaked my jeans. As I picked up the pace, I noticed a flashlight bobbing to the right of the inn.

"Hello!" I called.

The flashlight swiveled, shining right in my face. Then it went dark.

"Hello!" I called again, but there was no answer. My stomach tightened; who was skulking around the inn? I hurried to the kitchen door. As I mounted the steps, my right sneaker connected with something soft. I jerked back my foot and stepped over it, then pulled open the door.

Lying on the second step down was a small stuffed animal. Had someone dropped it? Or had someone left a stuffed animal on my front step intentionally? I looked over to where the flashlight had been, but there was only darkness.

I opened the door, and light flooded the drenched stones of the step... and the thing I had stepped on.

It was a stuffed animal with a rope noose around its neck.

My stomach churned as I bent for a closer look. It wasn't just any stuffed animal.

It was a ginger tabby.

11

I rushed into the house. "Biscuit! Smudge!" Neither cat was by the radiator, their favorite spot in the kitchen.

I slammed the kitchen door behind me and slid the deadbolt home, then hurried into the laundry room to where their food bowls were. No cats. I raced up the stairs, still calling their names, and pushed through into the bedroom.

To my relief, curled up in an orange and gray pile were Biscuit and Smudge, blinking sleepily and looking confused.

"Oh, thank God," I breathed, and sat down next to them, stroking their velvety heads. As they settled back down to sleep, both purring, I thought again about the gruesome offering on my step.

Mac had said just a few hours ago that curiosity killed the cat.

Was this his way of telling me he was serious?

I petted the cats a minute more until my heart rate dropped back into a manageable range, then headed downstairs to look for John.

He wasn't anywhere in the inn, and considering what I'd found on the doorstep, I wasn't comfortable walking out to the workshop. Instead, I grabbed my phone and dialed him.

My husband answered on the second ring. "What's up?"

"Someone left a stuffed animal in a noose on the front step," I told him.

"I'll be right there," he said. "Lock the doors. I have a key."

"Got it," I said. As I hung up, I hurried out to the front door and made sure it was secure, then jogged back to the kitchen. John was just coming in the back door as I entered, a baseball bat in his hand.

"Where is it?" he asked, his jaw set.

"On the step," I said, pointing to the kitchen door leading to the front of the inn.

He choked up on the bat with one hand and unlocked the door with the other. But when the door swung open, the stuffed animal was gone.

John looked at the empty step, then back at me.

"It was there five minutes ago. I swear."

He bent down and looked at the stone steps. "There's a dry spot here."

I exhaled. "So I'm not crazy."

"No," he said, peering into the darkness. "But whoever left it here is obviously nearby."

"Why come back to get it?"

"Since you found it, the threat has been delivered," John reasoned. "No reason to leave evidence."

"That's so creepy," I said.

"It is. And I'm going to see if I can find out who it is." He closed the door, pulled open the junk drawer and grabbed a flashlight, then pulled a jacket from a hook by the door.

"You can't go out there! It's not worth it!"

"Threats are unacceptable," he said. "Whoever did this is still out there. I'm going to see if I can track him—or her —down."

"I think you're crazy," I told him. "Stay."

"I'll take my phone," he said. "I'll call or text in a few minutes."

Before I could say anything else, he was gone.

I gripped my phone and watched through the window as John's flashlight bobbed into the woods, then disappeared. A series of unpleasant possibilities unfurled in my head as the rain lashed against the inn. What if whoever it was was armed with something other than a baseball bat? What if John never came back? I should have tried harder to keep him in the inn. If something were to happen to my husband...

As I stared into the darkness, a pair of headlights appeared at the top of the drive. As I watched, they bumped down the hill; it wasn't until the car turned in front of the inn that I recognized it as Murray's Jaguar. The Jag had barely come to a stop before the passenger door opened and Catherine spilled out, slamming the door behind her and marching to the kitchen door.

Murray jerked the car into reverse as Catherine unlocked the door and flung it open.

"Are you okay?" I asked as Murray skidded to a stop and then spun out as he headed up the driveway. I glanced toward the woods again; there was no sign of a flashlight. Was John all right?

"I don't want to talk about it," she said.

"Fine," I told her, "but please stay in the inn until John gets back."

She turned to look at me. Her eyes were red, her mascara smeared. I didn't think all the moisture on her face was from the rain. "Why?"

"Someone left something threatening on the doorstep. John's trying to track down whoever it was, but I don't want you to go to the carriage house alone."

Her blue eyes widened. "Something threatening? What was it?"

"A stuffed animal with a noose around its neck. It looked like Biscuit."

"Who would do something so horrible?" She looked around the kitchen. "And where is it?"

"Whoever left it came back and took it right after I saw it, we think. John's out looking for him."

"What? He went out alone?"

"I know," I told her. "He has a baseball bat, at least. I asked him not to, but he went out anyway. He's supposed to call me or text me." I stared down at my phone, willing something—anything—to appear. I glanced up at Catherine, who had gone pale. "Are you sure you're okay?"

"Murray broke up with me, and now my son is out there in the darkness with a madman or -woman on the loose..." She burst into tears and put her head in her hands.

"Oh, Catherine," I said, putting an arm on her damp shoulder. She turned to me, and I put my arms around her as she sobbed against me. "I'm so sorry."

"I just want my boy to be okay," she whispered. "Please let him be okay. Please, God. Please."

As if answering her prayer, my phone buzzed in my hand. I jerked up the phone above Catherine's shoulder so I could see the display. It was John.

"It's him," I said, reading the text. "He's okay."

"Thank God." She sagged in my arms.

"He lost the track. He's coming back to the inn."

"I need to sit down," she said, and I helped her over to

the kitchen table, then set myself to work making some tea. Tea always seemed to help. As I filled the teakettle with one eye still on the kitchen door, I said, "I'm here if you want to talk. And I understand if you don't."

"I don't know," she said. "Everything was going so well until that woman showed up. It turns out, the only reason he asked me out for tonight was that she wasn't going to be on the island."

I'd thought as much, but held my peace as I arranged some scones on a plate and fished two tea bags out of a canister.

"He's been two-timing me," she said bleakly. As she spoke, a flash of light darted across the driveway. I raced to the door just as John got there.

"You're okay?" I asked as I let him in.

"I lost the trail, but whoever it was dropped this," he said, tossing the limp stuffed animal on the kitchen counter.

"I'm so glad you're all right," Catherine said. "But what were you thinking, going out there in the dark? You could have been killed!"

"I'm the island deputy, remember?" he reminded her.

"I don't care," Catherine and I said in unison.

"It's not worth losing you," I said.

"She's right," Catherine said. "If whoever it was had a gun..."

"Exactly," I chimed in.

"On the plus side, now we have evidence," John said, changing the subject. "The noose was done with fishing line, which in my mind kind of points to an islander being responsible, not one of the guests." He registered the plate I'd been filling with baked goods. "Are those scones up for grabs?"

"They are," I replied. "And I'm making tea."

"Excellent," he said, helping himself to one. He looked at my mother-in-law. "How did it go with Murray?"

Catherine burst into tears and ran out of the kitchen.

"It hasn't been the best of days," I informed him as the door swung shut behind her.

THE RAIN WAS STILL PATTERING on the inn roof when I staggered out of bed the next morning, first checking to make sure Biscuit and Smudge were curled up next to John before heading downstairs to start the coffee. As I scooped beans into the grinder, I gazed out over the leaden water at the bottom of the hill; even the colorful buoys seemed dull in the gray light.

The sound of a boat engine thrummed in the distance as I checked first the front kitchen doorstep, then the back, relieved that there weren't any new "deliveries." As I closed the back door, I looked out at the sullen water; the *Island Queen* was chugging away from Cranberry Island toward the mainland after making its first stop for the day. I checked my recipe plan—crabmeat quiche with fruit salad and some of the scones I'd made yesterday—then scooped French roast beans into the grinder and measured out water, inhaling the scent of freshly ground coffee and looking forward to my first cup. I was just starting to measure out flour for the quiche crust when the phone rang.

It was Charlene. "What did you say to Gertrude?"

"What? What do you mean?"

"I'm looking at the *Daily Mail* right now. According to Gertrude, you named Adam Thrackton as a suspect."

I put down the measuring cup, scattering flour all over the kitchen and almost missing the counter. "What?"

"Apparently you claimed Chelsea was an undercover investigator, that Adam's catches have been suspiciously high lately, and that he may have sparked interest from regulatory agencies. You also named one of the artists as a suspect."

"I did no such thing," I said, and then an awful thought occurred to me. "Hang on a second, Charlene," I said. I pulled the phone away from my ear and went to recent calls. "Oh, no," I breathed as I looked at the call I'd made to the *Daily Mail* the day before. Although I'd left only a brief message, the length of the call was seven minutes.

I could hear Charlene's voice even with the phone in my hand. "What is it?"

I put the phone back to my ear. "Remember when I called Gertrude yesterday and left a message?"

"I do. You didn't say all the stuff in the article."

"I didn't hang up the phone," I said. "She heard every word we said in the store."

There was silence for a moment. "What all did we say?"

"Read the article," I said in a glum voice.

She was silent again. Then, in a slow voice, she said, "Well, fudge."

12

I swallowed hard, looking at the flour scattered on the counter. "Oh, Charlene. This is a horrible mistake. What do I do?"

"I don't know," she said. "Make a retraction? Say you were misquoted?"

"Can I even do that? Would she print it if I did? Clearly she's got my message recorded on her phone," I said, feeling almost sick to my stomach. "And what am I going to do about Adam and Gwen? When they read this... They're going to think I told Gertrude he's a suspect!"

"You'll have to explain it to both of them," she said. "I'm sure they know you'd never do anything to hurt them," she added in a weak voice.

"That makes one of us," I said. "Somebody left a nasty surprise on my doorstep, too." I filled her in on what I'd found the night before, and John's search of the woods.

"That's horrible! Do you think someone would really do something like that to Biscuit?"

"I don't let her outside," I said, "but I'm not always good about locking the door."

"You might want to start," she said.

"But the front door of the inn is always unlocked during the day."

"Lock her in your room when you're not there?" she suggested.

"That sounds miserable," I said, "but you're probably right. Better safe than sorry."

"Yes. Any word on what happened to Chelsea?"

"Not yet," I said, "but there is some other news. Murray and Catherine broke up."

"Oh, no," she said. "Who dropped the bomb?"

"I think Murray did."

"It's that Sarah woman, isn't it? They're together all the time."

"I think so," I said. "Catherine was pretty upset. By the way, how did it go with Robert?"

"Great, as always." I could hear the smile in her voice. "He's marvelous. He even ordered my favorite Cadbury chocolate from England!"

"I'm so glad," I said.

"Oh... hang on. Tom's here."

"Lockhart?"

"Yes."

"Can you swing by with a copy of the paper this morning?" I asked. "I've got guests."

"I don't have any coverage," she said. "Can you send John, or maybe he can cover?"

"I'll see what I can do," I said. "Tell me if you find anything out from Tom, okay?"

"I will," she promised, and hung up.

∾

BY THE TIME John came down, the piecrusts were in the oven and I was cutting up veggies to sauté.

"What smells so good?" he asked, rubbing his eyes and reaching for a coffee mug.

"I'm making quiche," I said. "Coffee's fresh. Could you make a quick run down to the store to pick up a copy of the *Daily Mail*?"

"What? Why?"

As I pulled the piecrusts out of the oven and sprinkled grated cheese on them, I explained to him what had happened.

He put down his mug. "You said that?"

"I don't remember what I said," I told him. "Eli told me he had had a lot of big catches lately, and that people down at the co-op were getting kind of suspicious. I know Adam had nothing to do with whatever happened to Chelsea."

"I'm going down to get that paper right now," he said. Without waiting for me to answer, he pulled on his boots and grabbed the keys to the van. "I'll be back in a minute."

"Thanks," I said, miserable. I wasn't sure I wanted to see what was in the paper. In fact, I knew I didn't want to see what was in the paper.

But I didn't really have a choice.

I glanced out the window at the water as I poured the veggies into a pan with melted butter. A lobster boat was chugging by the inn; by the buoy, I recognized it as Mac Penney's. A slight figure was bent over in the back: Josie Barefoot. Did she know where Mac had been when Chelsea disappeared? I recognized her close-cropped hair as she stood up and turned around. I'd seen her before; she had gone to high school on Mount Desert Island, but come back to live with her parents after graduation. How had she ended up sterning for Mac Penney? I wondered, giving the veggies a quick stir and then retrieving the eggs, half-and-half, and crabmeat from the fridge. I made a mental note to find out.

Catherine appeared as I finished whisking the half-and-half and eggs, looking like she hadn't slept a wink.

"He didn't call," she announced as she reached for a coffee mug and poured herself a cup. "I thought he'd have second thoughts. But he didn't."

"Give it time," I suggested.

She took a sip of black coffee and slumped into one of the kitchen chairs. "I don't think that will help."

"Want to talk about it?"

She paused for a moment, considering, and then the floodgates opened. "I shouldn't have said anything. I was just so upset about how much time he was spending with that Sarah woman. When I found out she was on the mainland, I accused Murray of only asking me to dinner because she wasn't available." She turned her mug around on the table; some of the dark liquid sloshed out onto the pine table, then she said in a bitter voice, "I told him if he wanted to spend all his time picking out carpet samples with some hussy he'd just met, I was done wasting my time."

"What did he say to that?" I asked.

"He said if that was how I felt about it, he'd take me home." She snorted. "On the way, he thanked me for the time we'd had together and said he hoped there were no hard feelings." She lifted the mug to her lips and took a mechanical sip. "I think it's over."

"I'm so sorry," I said.

"Don't be," she said. "I'd rather find out what he's really like sooner rather than later. I'll be just fine." Although she lifted her head regally, I could see the tears welling in her eyes. She took another sip of coffee and stood up. "I'm going down to my place. I'll be back to clean up after breakfast if you need me."

"Take the morning off," I suggested.

"No," she said quickly. "It'll do me good to stay busy."

"If you change your mind..."

"I'm fine," she said quickly, draining her coffee mug and yanking open the dishwasher. She jammed the mug into the top rack, slammed the door, and took another deep breath. "See you after breakfast," she announced, and then practically jogged to the back door.

It wasn't really any comfort at all, but at least I wasn't the only one having a crappy morning, I reflected as the door slammed behind her.

JOHN ROLLED BACK DOWN the hill in the van just as I was tucking the quiches into the oven. Although I loved the recipe, which was utterly decadent, with lumps of crabmeat encased in silky egg custard, my appetite had vanished; I might as well have been baking Styrofoam. He walked in as I closed the oven, the paper rolled up in his hand and a grim look on his tanned face.

I winced. "That bad?"

"That bad," he confirmed, handing me the paper. I read the article, which was above the fold on the front page, of course. Charlene had told me what it said, but seeing it in print made it ten times worse. I put it down, feeling sick to my stomach. "Gwen and Adam are going to kill me. What if I've accidentally made Adam a suspect?"

"I know Adam's innocent," John said. "I'm sure any investigation will bear that out." He walked over and put his hands on my shoulders. "I know you didn't mean to do it, but this is going to take some work to undo."

"I'm going to call the paper and retract it all."

"That's a start," he said. "If she'll print it."

"I feel awful," I said.

"I know," he said. "But it wasn't intentional. I'm sure they'll understand."

"I hope so," I replied, but I didn't feel so optimistic.

CHAD AND EMMA had just come down for breakfast when a yacht motored up outside the inn. My first thought was that it was Murray, come to visit Catherine with hat in hand, but it wasn't Murray's yacht. It was bigger, with black windows and a giant satellite dish on top of it. As I watched, a deck-hand tied it up at the pier; a moment later, a well-dressed couple disembarked, striding up my back path with purpose.

I didn't have any new guests booked for tonight, and even if I did, check-in wasn't until three. Still, I'd be happy to oblige if they needed a room... although the yacht looked like it had plenty of luxurious sleeping arrangements.

They mounted the steps to the back deck just as I opened the kitchen door.

"Good morning," I said. "Can I help you?"

"We're here to visit Chad," the woman said, smoothing her khaki skirt. A large diamond winked from her left hand; two of its cousins adorned her ears, and another hung from a delicate chain around her neck. Everything about her looked immaculately groomed, from her highlighted hair and French-manicured nails to her rather tight-looking face.

"Chad Berman," her companion—her husband, presumably—clarified. His wife was fit, but despite his tanned face and expensive-looking clothing—he wore khakis and a Polo shirt, and looked ready for a day at the golf course—he had a bit of a paunch over his slacks.

"He just came down, actually," I said. "Follow me; he's in the dining room."

They nodded without thanking me. I led them through the kitchen and pushed open the door to the dining room. Chad and Emma were sitting together in the corner. He had a coffee cup halfway to his lips when he spotted his parents. He put down the cup abruptly, a look of embarrassment— or shame?—flashing over his face.

He got up and hurried over to them, glancing back at Emma, who was watching the scene with curiosity in her bright eyes. I busied myself rearranging the buffet as they talked.

"What are you doing here?" he hissed.

"We read the article in the paper," his mother informed him, then glanced at me. "We don't think it's safe here. We're going to see about renting another place on the island; or maybe you can stay with us and we'll have David drop you off and pick you up."

I felt bad for Chad; he looked mortified.

"Mom. I'm fine."

"You're our only son," she said. "If something happened to you..."

"We're just taking reasonable precautions," his father interjected. "Now. We'll check you out; if you'll get packed today, we'll have you settled by this evening."

Chad glanced back at Emma, his face flushed.

"Can we talk outside?" he said in a low voice.

"I don't see what there is to talk about," his father said in a commanding voice. "We'll have the arrangements taken care of by the end of the day."

"I don't want to check out," Chad said. "Everything's fine. Someone did that girl in because she was investigating a lobster boat. It doesn't have anything to do with me."

"Sweetie, I still don't think it's a good idea to stay here. I'd sleep so much better if I knew you were somewhere safe."

Somewhere safe? Really?

"Get your things together," his father ordered. "We'll check out while you take care of it."

"I can't," Chad said. "I have to go to the Art Guild in twenty minutes. I said I'd be there by nine."

"Well, then, I'll take care of it," his mother said. She turned to me. "Um, Miss? Which room is he in?"

"Mom!" Chad said. "You can't just take over and tell me where to live."

"No?" his father said. "We're the primary investors in your little art concern. I think that gives us plenty of say."

"Charles," Chad's mother said, laying a hand on his arm. "We don't need to go there." She turned back to Chad. "Sweetie, go do what you need to do this morning. I'll take care of everything here; all I need is the key. By tonight, we'll have you somewhere safe, and likely twice as nice as this place."

I was torn between pity for Chad and fury for his parents, but kept my peace. I glanced over at Emma, who had obviously heard the whole exchange. Her mouth had quirked up a little bit, and again I felt bad for Chad, who didn't quite know what to do. Did he make a stand in front of Emma and risk alienating his parents? Or did he go along and face humiliation?

He opened his mouth, looking like he was going to tell them to get back onto their yacht and head back to the mainland, but before he could speak, his father said, "We only want what's best for you, Son."

Chad seemed to crumple. He handed the key to his mother. "It's on the second floor at the end," he told her.

Her face lit up. "Wonderful. I'll just go get started now." She turned to her husband. "You'll take care of the bill?"

"I'll handle it," he said as his wife planted a kiss on Chad's cheek and then patted him on the shoulder. "Now, go finish your breakfast with your friend, and we'll meet you at noon."

"Two," he said shortly.

"Okay. Two. We'll come get you at that art place, okay?"

"There's nowhere to dock," he pointed out.

She sighed. "I'll walk over, and we can walk back together."

"Fine," he said, and turned back to the table where Emma suddenly busied herself cutting into her quiche.

"Now, then," Chad's father said. "I need to settle up."

"Follow me," I said, leading him to the front desk as his wife marched toward the stairs. He pulled out an American Express Platinum Card and barely looked at the bill before signing it with a flourish. "I'll have a cup of coffee while I wait," he informed me.

I resisted the urge to tell him to go jump off his yacht. Not only was he rude, but he and his wife had just talked their son out of giving me another month of booking income... income I'd been counting on. And considering what had been printed in the *Daily Mail* this morning, I wasn't exactly in a good position to talk to Gwen about doing co-op advertising. So instead of whacking Mr. Berman Senior over the head with a stapler—the urge was strong—I put on as polite a smile as I could muster and directed him to the dining room. As he turned from the front desk, Noelle and Bruce sauntered down the stairs, hand in hand. Whatever had been bothering them seemed to have cleared up; at least someone was having a decent day.

"What's for breakfast?" Noelle asked.

"Crabmeat quiche," I said.

"Ooh, that sounds delicious," Noelle said, pushing a lock of hair behind her ear.

"Find a table and I'll bring you some coffee," I said.

"Hey, did they ever find out what happened to that girl?" Bruce asked.

"No," I said.

"The police asked a lot of questions," he said.

"I'm sure it's just routine," I said. "I'll bring you breakfast in a minute; feel free to find a table."

"Thanks," Noelle said with a smile, then nuzzled into Bruce again. As they seated themselves by a window, I hurried back into the kitchen. I grabbed three coffee cups and the coffee carafe and headed back into the dining room, delivering two to Bruce and Noelle and one to Chad's father, who was already on his cell phone and completely ignored me as I set the mug in front of him. I had to wave to catch his attention.

"What?" he asked sharply.

"We don't allow cell phones in the dining room, I'm afraid," I told him. "You are welcome to take your coffee out on the deck."

"I'll only be a minute," he said, and went back to his conversation.

"No," I said. "You'll have to take it outside. It's disturbing my guests."

"Give me just a second, Richard, okay?" he said into the phone, then hit the Hold button.

"Is there a problem?"

"Like I said, we don't allow cell phones in the dining room. You'll have to take it outside."

He sighed and went back to his call. "Sorry. This woman is giving me a hard time about the phone. What time are you thinking? Noon? I think I can do that. Yeah, we'll go down to the club for lunch afterward. Absolutely. See you then. Say hi to Midge for me!" When he was done, he looked at me. "There. All done."

I gave him a tight smile and walked away.

"Where are the cream and sugar?" he asked.

"Over there," I said, pointing to the buffet, and continued to the kitchen.

The phone rang as soon as the door swung shut behind me. I stared at the phone as if it were a poisonous snake—I'd left a message for Gwen first thing, and was dreading the return call—then picked it up.

"Gray Whale Inn, can I help you?"

"How could you?" It was Gwen, sounding angrier than I'd ever heard her.

13

*A*nd that was saying something, as she and her mother, my sister, had quite a history. I winced.

"I'm so sorry," I said. "I can explain..."

"You'd better start," she said. "Although I'm not sure how you're going to make it any better. I can't believe you told Gertrude that about Adam!"

"I didn't," I said. "I called her to leave a message and must have accidentally not hung up. She overheard my conversation."

"That still means you told someone Adam was a suspect."

"I was only reporting what I heard from someone else," I said. "I don't believe Adam had anything to do with this. Do you think I'd encourage my niece to marry someone I thought was capable of murder?"

She was quiet for a moment.

"I left a message for Gertrude the moment I saw the article," I told her. "I'm trying to get her to print a retraction. I know it's not the same as never printing it at all, but I'm doing everything I can to fix it."

"Good," she said, taking a deep breath. "I'll try to explain it to Adam. But it still doesn't make it better."

"I know, honey," I told her. "I'm so sorry this happened. It's my fault. I'll do anything I can to make it up to you."

"How about finding the actual murderer, so people stop talking about us?"

"I'll do my best," I told her.

She sighed. "I know you'd never do anything like that intentionally, but... I still can't believe you said it."

"I'm sorry," I repeated.

"I'll think about it," she told me. "Anyway, I guess I'll see you later. I've got to run. Bye."

"Goodbye," I replied, but she had already hung up.

I put down the phone and cut two more pieces of quiche with a heavy heart. I couldn't believe what a mess I'd made of things.

EMMA LINGERED a few minutes after everyone else had left. She was sipping her coffee and sketching the scene from the window, using the window itself as a frame. As I cleared the last of the tables, she said, "What do you think of Chad Berman?"

I glanced over at her, surprised by the direct question.

"He certainly seems intrigued by you," I said.

"It's not me he's intrigued by," she said dryly, adding another line to her sketch. "It's what I do that interests him."

"Your art? But he's an artist, too," I said.

She shrugged. "He makes things with clay. But to do art takes work," she said simply.

"I always thought it was about talent."

"Talent can only take you so far," she replied. "Effort and

time are key. It doesn't just happen." She waved a hand. "Did this inn just happen?"

As I picked up the coffee carafe and wiped a small spill, I thought about the risk I'd taken to come here, pouring my life savings into this historic building at the edge of Maine, and the continued worries I had about keeping the business healthy. "No," I said.

She leaned forward and looked at me. "You worked at it. You still do."

"That's true," I said.

"What did you do before you were an innkeeper?" she asked.

"I worked for the Parks and Wildlife Department in Austin, Texas," I told her.

"You really wanted to do this, didn't you?" she asked. Her eyes were intense. "This place spoke to you, and you risked a lot to answer the call."

"I did," I said, taken aback by her insight.

She nodded. "I did too. My parents wanted me to do an accounting degree. Practical. Lucrative." She put down the cup. "Safe."

She sounded like my niece, who had defied my sister to pursue art as a career. "But you didn't."

Emma shook her head. "I didn't. And I paid the price for that for a while. My paintings never sold for much for years. I ate beans and rice, I shared a house on the wrong side of the tracks just so I could afford the rent, but I never stopped sketching, never stopped painting, never stopped learning."

"You're doing well now," I said. I'd seen the price tags on her paintings at the Guild. And I knew at least half of them had sold, and the summer had just begun.

"I am," she said. "But I sacrificed for it. Chad doesn't understand that. He just expects it to 'happen.'"

"I can see that."

"I looked up his work when I first met him."

"Oh?"

"He started with woodworking, but he decided the medium 'wasn't for him.' Then he worked with collage, but after six months decided it was too 'limiting.' Now it's pottery, and... well, he hasn't taken the time to really learn the medium, but he's disappointed his sales aren't better."

"He doesn't need the money."

"It's not the money," she said. "It's the stamp of approval the money means."

"I see," I said. "He's interested in what you're doing."

"He is. He's seen that my work is in demand, so he's thinking if he tries oil painting, that will be the answer."

"Looking for the magic bullet."

"Exactly. But what he doesn't understand," she said, "is that you do it because you have to. The money is nice, and necessary to live on, but that's not what keeps you going." She sipped her coffee and stared out at the water. "You do it because there's something that's yearning to come out that he's got to try again and again to make a reality. He may have that somewhere, but he hasn't found it. It's not what's driving him."

"No?"

She shook her head. "It's recognition he wants."

"So there's no hope for him?"

"I didn't say that," she said, glancing at me with an arched eyebrow. "There's always hope. But he's got a few things working against him."

"Like the folks who showed up earlier, you mean?"

She nodded. "They make it too easy for him. They smooth everything out. Keep him from feeling any hardship." She made another few lines on the page. "He has to close out the world and listen to what's inside, instead of trying to look a certain way, or please his parents, or work for approval."

"I can see that," I said, thinking of my niece's struggle.

"Ironically, the way for him to get the approval he wants is for him not to want it."

"Kind of a sticky wicket, isn't it?"

"It is," she mused, then put another few lines on her sketch. "It's complicated doing art for a living."

"It sounds like it," I said.

"Your niece knows what she's doing," she informed me. "So does your husband. They do their work for the right reasons. And they work hard. It shines through in their pieces."

I felt myself glow with pride. "Thank you for saying so," I told her. "I feel the same way."

"And so do you," she added, glancing around at the dining room. "This is your art. You've created a place. This inn is your work."

"I'd never thought of it that way, but... I think you're right," I said, looking around at the pine tables, the scones in a basket on the buffet, the sea glass sparkling in a Mason jar on the windowsill. "Ever have moments of doubt?" I asked, thinking of my low bookings and my worries about the future.

"All the time," she said. "But I push through anyway."

"Of course you do," I said. As I spoke, she tore off the sketch and handed it to me. "View from your dining-room window on a cloudy morning," she said. "For you."

"Thank you," I said as she packed up her things.

"My pleasure," she told me, smiling. "Thank you for creating this beautiful place. I'm thinking of trying something new... and I don't think it would have occurred to me if I hadn't stayed here."

"Like what?" I asked.

"You'll see," she said. "Thank you for breakfast. And for the conversation."

"Likewise," I said. "You've given me a lot to think about."

As she tucked her notebook into her bag, she said, "Watch out for those people."

"What people?"

"Chad's parents," she said. "I have a bad feeling about them. And my feelings are usually right." And with that, she walked out of the dining room.

AFTER I'D FINISHED the last of the cleanup, I called Gertrude again, but there was still no answer, so I left another message. John had gone down to his workshop, and I had no idea where Catherine was. Feeling at loose ends, I decided to start another scone recipe; the deadline for submitting the recipe was next week, and I was still trying to come up with something spectacular.

I opened the fridge to see what I had. John had picked up groceries at the store, so we now had lemons, along with a flat of wild blueberries. Lemon scones with blueberries might work; I'd made muffins with that combination, but never scones. With a lemon glaze, they could be sensational.

I flipped through my binder to find a basic scone recipe, then turned on the oven and set to work. As I gathered ingredients, I thought about Chelsea, and who might have wanted to do her harm.

She and Chad obviously had some background, so there

was at least one person who knew her before she came to the island. And if she was in fact an investigator—or if people thought she was one—it was in the interest of any lobsterman who was up to no good to have her out of the way. Mac was the obvious suspect—after all, he had not only threatened Earl, but bashed in his boat—but what about Earl himself? He had a secret compartment in the *Lucky Lady*, after all.

But if his boat was in dry dock when Chelsea arrived on the island to observe—or potentially investigate—fishing infractions, what motive would he have for killing her? You can't get caught if you're not fishing, after all.

As I measured out flour and poured it into a bowl, my mind turned back to Chelsea. She'd shown up for breakfast, then left quickly after her run-in with Chad. Either whoever encountered her on the path knew she was going that way or was spying on the inn and followed her when she left. Was it possible that Mac was lying in wait for her? Maybe he'd watched for her to leave the inn, then followed her and killed her once she was out of sight of prying eyes?

I knew most lobstermen were out on their boats early, but with the mooring lines cut, no one would have been out on the water. I knew a lobsterman usually worked with a sternman. Mac worked with Josie Barefoot. Even thought they hadn't been out on the water, she might know where Mac was when Chelsea died. I made a mental note to find out where Earl was, too... just to cover all the bases.

I zested a lemon and added the zest to the dry ingredients, then cut in the butter. The rhythmic movement calmed me. I thought again about my mistake with Gertrude, and turned my mind to potential suspects.

It could have been any of the lobstermen on the island, but there were options at the inn, too. Chelsea and Chad

had had a run-in in the past. Had Chad's hurt feelings been enough to make him do in his old classmate?

Or was there some other piece of history there I didn't know about?

On a whim, I added vanilla to the cream and egg I'd just whisked up before pouring them into the dry mixture. I'd saved the juice for the glaze so it wouldn't interfere with the rising of the dough. I measured out blueberries, gently kneading them into the dough, and then jotted down the proportions so I wouldn't forget.

As I worked the dough into a rough circle, my eye fell on the bedraggled stuffed animal I'd found on the doorstep last night. Instinctively, I checked the window where Biscuit and Smudge liked to lie in the sun; thankfully, both were there, but I didn't like the threat. The cats usually enjoyed their indoor/outdoor independence, but John and I had decided to enforce indoor quarantine until we figured out who had left that horrible thing on our doorstep. But how would we figure it out? There wasn't a lot to go on.

And what was the reason for the threat?

I didn't know, but I did know I wanted to talk to Josie Barefoot, Mac Penney's sternman. And to Tom Lockhart, to see if he had any more insight as to what all was going on down at the co-op. And I was still waiting for news on Claudette's tests.

The phone rang, and I sighed, wondering what it could be now. Adam? Eli? It had not been a good week, I thought to myself as I wiped my hands and reached for the phone.

"Hello?"

Breathing. There was the faint sound of a boat motor in the background.

"Hello?"

More breathing. And then a click.

14

*G*oose bumps rose on my arms as I pulled the phone away from my ear and checked the Caller ID. Whoever had called had blocked the number.

It had been years since I'd received a prank call. Was that what this was?

Or was it related to what I had found on my porch the night before?

My meditative mood shattered, I cut the scones and put them on a parchment-paper-lined baking sheet, then slid them into the oven and checked the locks on the doors again, then pushed through the door to the dining room, intending to head to the front door to make sure it was locked, too; I didn't usually go to such measures, but right now, I was being very careful.

I was about to round the corner into the parlor when I heard voices.

"I told you. We're fine."

"Are you sure?" The first voice was low and male, the second female and anxious. "What if she told someone?"

"Who would she tell? No one here knows us."

"I don't mean here," the woman said. "I mean back home."

"Who would she tell?" the man asked again. "We don't run in the same circles. We're only acquaintances; it's not like we were best friends, or like she had phone numbers or anything."

"She might have called," the woman protested. "Looked up the numbers online."

"The service here is so spotty, I don't see how she could. Besides, she only had what, a half hour? You worry too much."

"If it got out, I don't know what I'd do. Oh, God. I knew this was a bad idea."

"We're fine. No one will know."

"I don't know. I shouldn't have agreed to this. I'm so stupid... this was such a bad idea."

"Noelle..."

"I need to be alone," she said. "I need to think."

Footsteps sounded, and then came the squeak of a door opening. I retreated to the kitchen door, and was just about to slip through it when Bruce rounded the corner, looking angry and unhappy. His eyes narrowed when he saw me.

"Oh, hi," I said. "Can I get you anything?"

"How long have you been here?" he asked.

"Been where?" I asked. "I've been in the kitchen making scones. They'll be out in a bit if you're hungry. I was just about to check to make sure the front door was locked."

He stared at me, as if sizing me up.

"Is something wrong?" I asked.

"No," he said slowly. "It's fine."

"Good," I said, bustling past him. "Let me know if you need anything. And like I said, scones will be out in a bit."

"I'm not hungry, but thanks," he said. "And don't lock the door yet. I'm going for a walk."

"Sure," I said, oddly thankful that he'd be leaving the inn. There was something deeply unsettling about Bruce at the moment: agitated, brooding. Potentially violent?

As he let himself out the front door, I headed to the front desk and pulled up the bookings screen, thinking of what he and Noelle had been talking about. What were they worried about someone—presumably Chelsea, based on Bruce's timing comment—seeing?

I looked up the home addresses of Bruce and Noelle. Both were from a suburb a little bit north of Portland. Then I pulled up Chelsea's address.

Same neighborhood.

I glanced up to make sure I was alone and then pulled up Noelle's Facebook page. Her profile picture showed her with two black-haired children and a man I didn't recognize.

A quick look at Bruce's profile confirmed what I suspected. Both Noelle and Bruce were married. Just not to each other.

I closed the window and thought about Chelsea. She'd died a half hour after spotting Bruce and Noelle. Had one of them decided to get rid of her before she could break the news back home?

THE SCONES HAD JUST COME out of the oven when John appeared at the kitchen door. "Everything here okay?" he asked first.

"No more threats," I said. "Biscuit and Smudge are up in the bedroom. And no more murders, at least as far as I know."

"Good," he said.

"There was a weird phone call, though," I said as I transferred the scones from the pan to a cooling rack.

"What kind of weird phone call?" he asked.

As I laid another scone on the cooling rack, I told him about the breathing.

"Did you get a number?"

"Anonymous," I said. "I don't know if it has anything to do with the stuffed cat on the porch, but it was creepy."

"It was," he said. "Maybe I need to spend more time in the inn with you until this gets figured out."

"I'm sure I'll be fine," I said, transferring the last of the scones to the rack and then giving the glaze I'd made while they were baking a whisk. "Want one? It's an experimental recipe."

"They smell amazing," he said. "How can I say no?"

As I put a scone on a plate, adding a dollop of glaze as John poured himself a glass of milk, I relayed what I'd overheard between Bruce and Noelle... and what I'd found on Facebook.

"And she died right after she spotted them," John said, echoing my thoughts from earlier. "This is amazing, by the way," he said, wiping a bit of glaze from his chin.

"Good enough to enter in the contest?"

"I'd give them a blue ribbon for sure. Don't let me keep you from continuing to experiment, though."

"Well, at least one thing is going right."

He swallowed another bite and said, "You really think Bruce and Noelle might have had something to do with Chelsea?"

"Maybe it's far-fetched," I told him, "but I think it's worth thinking about. I knew she knew Chad, but I can't think of what would cause him to murder her. If anything, you'd think it would be the other way around; after all, he's the one with the silver spoon in his mouth."

"He didn't stand to gain much from killing her," John agreed.

"But what about Mac and Earl?" I asked.

"I assume they were marooned on the island when she died," he said.

"Which leaves us with a rather extensive suspect list." I grimaced. "You don't think they'll go after Adam, do you?"

"You're worried about that quote, aren't you?"

"I talked with Gwen and tried to settle things down, but... I'm worried. Have you talked to the investigators at all?"

"I told them about the stuffed animal, but I doubt they'll follow up on it. I know they talked with all the artists and the guests, but they haven't told me if they've got anything they consider a good lead. I'll tell them about Bruce and Noelle, though."

"That'll make me popular," I said.

"I won't mention that it came from you," he said.

"Bruce knows I overheard them talking. I'm married to you. How hard do you think it'll be for them to figure it out?"

"You do have a point."

"On the other hand," I said as I took a corner of scone for myself, "the first priority is finding out what happened to poor Chelsea."

"And making sure it doesn't happen again," John added in an ominous tone.

~

ONCE THE KITCHEN was cleaned up, I had a few hours before it was time to get dinner going, so I decided to head out to see if I could chat with Mac's sternman, Josie Barefoot.

Charlene had told me she was living in a carriage house behind one of the old captain's houses close to the pier. The Boston family that owned the big house hadn't come up for the summer yet, but Josie was renting the carriage house from them and keeping an eye on the property for a discount.

It was a beautiful day for a walk; the sun was out, and it was hard to imagine that anyone could harbor murderous impulses. Normally, I'd take the cliff path and enjoy the view of the water, but after finding Chelsea, I couldn't bring myself to walk that way. Besides, after the macabre deposit on my doorstep and the anonymous phone call, I was still on guard. Despite the sweet smell of balsam fir tinged with salt air, every time a breeze rustled the grass along the road, I found myself glancing over my shoulder. I was definitely jumpy.

I'd just crested the hill when I ran into Lorraine Lockhart. "Natalie!" she called, shading her eyes and waving. "I was hoping I might run into you."

"What's up?"

"Tom wants to talk to John," she said. "I don't know if you've heard, but someone's been messing with the boats down at the co-op."

"I did hear," I said. "Any luck finding them all?"

"All but Adam's," she said.

"How bad's the damage?"

"A few are pretty banged up, but miraculously, none of them have sunk. Presuming we find the *Carpe Diem*," she said, referring to Adam's boat.

"Does Tom want John to look into it?"

She nodded. "Tempers have been pretty high here lately, as I'm sure you know. Tom's hoping we can take care of things among ourselves."

"I get that," I said. "But things seem to be escalating."

"Are you talking about that young woman? This has nothing to do with her. I heard she fell and hit her head."

"Maybe," I said. "But if she didn't, we may have a murderer running loose on the island. If that's the case, it might not be so bad to get the Marine Patrol on board."

She sucked in her breath. "If it comes to it, I guess... but let's see what we can do first."

"Got it," I said. "I'll tell John when I see him."

"Thanks," she said.

"Say hi to the kids for me!" I told her as she moved on.

"I will!" she called, but she didn't sound chirpy.

Why was Tom so adamant about not calling in the Marine Patrol? I wondered.

Did he have something to hide?

I was still ruminating when I got to the tall yellow house at the top of the hill by the pier. It had a full view of the small harbor, and I could almost imagine the former captain's wife at the top window, scanning the water for the return of her husband's vessel.

Although the curtains of the yellow house were all closed, music with a heavy beat was emanating from the small house behind it. I had to knock twice before the volume dropped; a moment later, the door opened, and I was facing a surprised-looking young woman in cutoff shorts and a faded University of Maine sweatshirt. Her hair was cut short and shaved on the sides; the style accentuated her high cheekbones and angular jaw.

"Hey," she said. "Are you looking for the Wakefields? They're not here for another week."

"No," I said. "I think I'm looking for you. You're Josie, right?" I stuck out a hand. "I'm Natalie. I own the Gray Whale Inn."

"Right," she said, shaking my hand with a firm grip but looking perplexed. "But why are you looking for me?"

"You're Mac Penney's sternman, right?"

"I am," she said, looking wary. "Why?"

"I was hoping you could tell me a little about Mac," I said.

"I'm not so sure I should talk about my employer," she told me. Her eyes were steady on mine, but wary. "I need the job."

"Something happened to a young woman by the inn," I said. "She was supposed to go out on Mac's boat. I'm not trying to go after your employer; I'm just trying to find out what happened." I paused; she made no move to open the door wider. "A young woman died," I said. "I want to make sure that doesn't happen again."

She scanned the area behind me. "No one knows you're here?"

"No one," I confirmed. "And I won't say anything to anyone."

She stood still for a moment, then appeared to make a decision. "Come in fast," she said, stepping back. "Before someone sees you."

15

I hurried through the door and she closed it behind her, peeking through the windows at the top of the door. "I should know better, really. There aren't any secrets on this island. And I need this job."

"I appreciate it," I said.

"I don't know if I'll be any help, but I'll do what I can," she said. "Can I get you a drink? Tea, water, coffee? I'm on short rations at the moment, I'm afraid; I'm trying to save for school."

"Just water would be great," I said.

"Go ahead, sit down," she told me, pointing to the two wooden chairs flanking a small Formica table. As I sat down, I glanced around the house. A small single bed, neatly made with what looked like a handmade quilt, stood in one corner under a window, with a crate functioning as a nightstand beside it. A slightly saggy beige couch was pushed up against the wall perpendicular to the bed; it faced a scarred wood dresser with a small, tube-style TV on top of it. The kitchen, which was on the wall next to the front door, consisted of a sink, two burners, a toaster oven, a dorm-size fridge, a microwave, and the table I was sitting at. The floor was scarred stained wood, with red rag rugs under the kitchen table and next to the bed. A door at the far end led, presumably, to a bathroom. It was small, but clean and tidy, with lots of windows and good light.

As I watched, Josie filled two glasses, fished a few ice cubes out of the metal tray she retrieved from the tiny freezer shelf in the fridge, and set them on the table.

"Thanks," I said, taking a sip.

"Sure."

"Out of curiosity, what are you studying?"

"Marine biology and environmental science," she told me.

"What made you decide to work on the island for the summer?"

"It's good money. Plus, I like the sea. And it's a good opportunity to see how the fishery really works."

"Does Mac know what you're studying?"

She grinned. "I didn't mention it to him, no; I don't think he's too pro-conservation. I just told him I'm a hard worker. I don't think he had too many other applications for the job. He's not the friendliest lobsterman on the island."

"It's hard work."

"It is," she said. "But it keeps me fit. I'm on the crew team during the school year, so the work suits me."

"It sounds like you like it."

"I do," she said, taking a sip of her water. "I'm hoping the boat will be fixed up and we can be back out tomorrow. I love the water, and I love the rhythm of it. Mac isn't a big talker, so we do the work and keep the chat to a minimum."

"Were you around when the... uh, incident happened?"

"What? With Earl's boat?" She shook her head. "I'd

already gone home for the night. I don't know what the man was thinking. Probably had too many Pabst Blue Ribbons."

"Did he ever drink while you were out with him?"

She hesitated, then nodded. "He thought I didn't see. Kept it in a thermos. But I did." She took another sip of water. "I kept a close eye on him when he was at the helm."

"I'll bet," I said. "I hate to ask, but... do you know if he was doing anything he shouldn't have been doing?"

She bit her lip. "Not while I was on board," she said. "But he went out without me sometimes. I saw him a few times."

"Was anyone with him?"

She nodded.

"Who?"

"I don't know," she said. "He went out alone when he went, but once I saw him out right around sunset with someone else on the boat. I asked him about it, but he didn't say who it was. They were headed away from the mainland."

"Fishing?"

"Maybe," she said.

"Or something else?"

"The only thing I ever saw him do was fish," she said.

"I understand," I told her. "The morning I found Chelsea... were you with Mac down at the co-op?"

"I was," she said. "But I met him at six and was home by seven. Hard to work when there's no boat."

"Was Mac there when you left?"

"He wasn't," she said. "He said something about sticking an oar in where it doesn't belong and stormed off into the woods. It's a good thing Earl's boat was in dry dock after being rammed or I think Mac might have gone after it again."

"Bad blood there?"

"I don't know why, but Mac's got it in for Earl. Anyway,

Tom was busy getting the remaining boats to go search for the ones whose lines were cut. I offered to help, but they had more than enough people already, so I came home."

"Did you see or talk to Mac at all later that morning?"

Josie shook her head. "I didn't see him until late afternoon, when I went down to the co-op to see what was going on." She grimaced. "He was about half a case down by then and not too coherent."

"Do you know if he met Chelsea at all? The woman who was going to be on the boat?"

She shook her head. "He knew what she looked like, though. Everyone did. It was all on the radio that the investigator was a young woman with black hair. They were talking about being surprised she was so young."

"They thought she was an investigator? I heard she was just an observer."

Josie rolled her eyes. "Nobody believed that. There've been too many rumors about illegal fishing on Cranberry Island lately. Even folks on the mainland are talking about it. Tom's been trying to keep things on the down-low, but after what happened yesterday..." She ran a hand through her dark hair and shook her head. "I wish him luck."

"Was there a lot of talk about her, then?"

"Of course there was," she said. "What else is there to do? But it was mainly speculation."

"Anyone threaten her?"

She shrugged. "Oh, I heard a bit of talk, but I didn't take it too seriously.

"Who threatened her, if you remember?"

"Well, Mac, of course. But he was always threatening people. Mainly Earl." She turned her glass around on the table, making a wet ring I had an urge to wipe up. "I don't know what was up between them. For all they hated each other, I saw them talking with their heads down more than once, like they were best friends or something."

"What were they talking about?" I asked.

"Who knows? I was too far away to hear. They've both lived on this island most of their lives. They've got that in common, at least."

I leaned forward. "It may seem like a direct question, but... do you think Mac would have been capable of killing Chelsea?"

She leaned back in her chair and crossed her arms over the University of Maine logo. "Capable?" She considered the question for a moment before answering. "I don't know if he's capable of it. But he's not a soft man. And he hates regulation, and she certainly was linked with regulation."

"Is it possible he was afraid she might find something if she went out on his boat?"

She turned her glass around some more as she thought about it. "I don't know," she said finally. "I never saw anything out of place, although he kept some compartments locked when I was on board. Still," she added, glancing up at me, "it is an odd coincidence that half the fleet should be cut loose the night before the observer was scheduled to be on board one of them."

"And a bigger coincidence that Mac's boat is still missing," I pointed out.

"That fact hadn't escaped me. Maybe he did cut them all loose. Even his own."

"Or else he hid his away and cut the others as a cover story," I suggested. "The question is—and I know this is all speculation—if he did, why?"

"Your guess is as good as mine," Josie said. "All I know is, I hope he's back in business soon or I'm going to have to find a job on the island."

"If you need something to tide you over, I could always do with some help at the inn. You seem smart and capable."

"Thanks," she said, taking another swig of water. "If we're not up and running in the next day or two, I might take you up on it. What kind of work?"

"How are you with computers and marketing?" I asked.

"I know a little bit about it," she said. "My last summer job was at a social media marketing agency."

"Really?"

"Really," she said. "I'm not quite an expert, but I learned a few things that might help."

"No offense, but I'm kind of hoping Mac doesn't find his boat," I said half-jokingly. "I could use you!"

"Well, even if he does find it, I've got a few hours off from time to time. Want me to stop by to talk to you about it sometime?"

"That would be great," I said, digging in my wallet for a card. "Anytime. And thanks so much for talking to me," I said as we both stood up. "If there's anything at all you can think of about Mac or Chelsea or anything, please let me know."

"I'm curious: Does your interest have to do with the unfortunate article in the *Daily Mail*, or is it something else?" Josie asked as I took another sip of water.

"I'm upset about the article, of course," I said, "but I'm more upset that someone ended a young woman's life. And I'd like to make sure it doesn't happen again." I put my glass in the sink. "I'd tell you to be careful, but I can tell you know how to take care of yourself."

"I'm always careful," she confirmed. "And I appreciate your concern." As she walked me to the door, she stopped suddenly. "Wait," she said.

I turned. "What?"

"I just remembered something," she said. "He made some comment to Earl about how there was originally going to be a snow day, but the weather report changed."

"Snow day?" I asked. "It's a little late in the year for that, even in Maine."

"I know," she said. "I don't know if it means anything. I just thought it was weird. Anyway, I may be by tomorrow, if that works for you."

"That would be great," I said. "Hope to see you then." I reached for the doorknob, then paused. "Want me to go out the back door in case someone sees me?"

"There is no back door," she pointed out. "Besides, now that you're interviewing me for a job, I've got a cover story."

"Right," I said. "Thanks again. I hope to see you tomorrow! And if you remember anything else..."

"I'll let you know," she said with a grin.

ON THE WAY back to the inn, I swung by Eli and Claudette's house. Eli, as usual, was at work in the barn next to the house; I could hear the sound of power tools before I even crossed the boat-strewn meadow. I waved as I stepped into the barn; Eli was crouched at the front of the *Lucky Lady*, which was looking a lot more whole than the last time I'd seen her.

"How goes it?" I asked as he powered down the sander and took off his goggles.

"Almost done with this girl," he said, patting the boat's hull.

"Good thing, since from what I hear, you're going to have a lot more customers soon."

"True," he said.

"How's Claudette?"

He grimaced. "The test results are back in."

"And?"

"They won't tell us until her appointment tomorrow," he said. "Which to my mind means there's something they'll have to tell us. Of course, I didn't say that to Claudie, but she knows, too."

"I'm so sorry," I said.

"I asked if she wanted anyone else to come, and she said no. Wants it to be just us."

"I understand... I'm here if you need me, though. And even if they did find something, maybe it's not as bad as you're thinking."

"Maybe," he said dolefully.

"You know I'm happy to go with you if you need a second pair of ears, or even just moral support."

"I know," he said, "but Claudie doesn't want it."

"I understand," I told him. "But I'm here if you need me."

"Thanks," he said. "Saw what ended up in the *Daily Mail*," he continued, changing the subject. "Heard from Adam yet?"

"No, but I got an earful from Gwen. I must not have hung up when I left Gertrude a message, and she listened to the conversation we had at the store."

"At least she's still speaking with you, I suppose," said Eli. "The faster they find that killer, the faster this will all blow over."

"I know," I said. "I'd also like to make sure nobody else dies."

"There is that," he agreed.

"You must have talked to some of the lobstermen," I said. "Any interesting rumors to report?"

He looked at me for a long moment, then said, "Someone's up to something squirrelly."

"What do you mean?"

"There's something most everyone knows but no one's talking about. I think some of 'em are in the dark, but I get the feelin' not everyone is."

"Tom Lockhart, too?" I asked.

"He's tryin' to keep the Marine Patrol out of things, that's for sure. I don't know if that means he's in on whatever they're up to, or he's just tryin' to protect the island."

"Who do you think is involved in whatever's going on?"

He looked around, as if someone might be eavesdropping. "I don't like to talk out of school."

"I know," I said. "I won't tell anyone you said anything to me."

"Won't matter. Everyone knows we're friends." He looked worried. "All right. Mac and Earl are up to something. I'm sure of it."

"I heard something about that," I said.

"And I hate to say it... but Adam's been shiftylike lately. Goin' out extra time. Big hauls, too... people are talkin'."

"You mentioned that," I said. "What do you think?"

"I don't know," he said. "But I do think Earl might be fishing hidden traps."

"Because of the compartment you found?" I asked.

He nodded.

"But why would he and Mac be in on it? And if they were, why would Mac accuse Earl of snitching on him?"

"Makes no sense to me either," he said. "But somethin's goin' on."

"It takes two people to run a lobster boat, doesn't it?"

"Ayuh."

"Maybe they were fishing illegally together? Taking out the boat at night to pull traps?"

"It's possible," Eli said. "But like you said, why would Earl snitch?"

"I don't know," I said. "Maybe he didn't. Maybe Mac just thought he did. Maybe he just drank too much and got mad."

"That has been known to happen," he said. "From what I hear, he's been hittin' the bottle a bit much lately."

"Or the can," I said, thinking of the case of PBR he had picked up at the store. "By the way, have you had any weird things happen lately?"

"Weird? Like what?"

I told him what I'd found on my doorstep the day before.

"Nothin' like that here," he said. "Your kitties okay?"

"So far," I told him. "I've been extra-careful to keep them in. I don't know why anyone would threaten them, though."

"I think the threat was for you, my dear. You do tend to stick your nose into things, if you don't mind my sayin'," he pointed out. "Particularly when your guests are involved."

"Someone's trying to warn me off," I said.

"Not workin', is it?" he pointed out.

"Not really," I said.

"You're like a terrier with a bone," he said. "You don't give up."

"No," I said.

"By the way, who was in that pretty yacht that pulled up outside the inn?"

"You saw it?"

"I did. I heard from Charlene that John told her it belonged to one of those artists, but I can't see anything down at the Guild makin' enough to pay for that kind of boat."

"It's the parents'," I clarified. "The parents of one of the artists is funding most of the Guild. After what happened to the observer, they decided the inn wasn't a safe place for their little boy, so they're renting him a house on the island, instead."

"How old is this artist?" he asked.

"Midtwenties, I think."

He took off his cap and shook his head. "I'd been earnin' a livin' buildin' boats for a decade by the time I hit twenty-five," he said. "Can't imagine my parents sweepin' in and runnin' my life at that age."

I'd had the same thought. "He did look rather embarrassed," I said.

"He should've told 'em to go take a flyin' leap, if you want my opinion."

"They were paying the bill, so I don't think he could," I said. "I don't think his art is particularly profitable."

"Which art is it?" he asked.

"The clay sea creatures. The artist is Chad Berman."

"You mean those black globs?" He snorted. "My grandson made a pot in preschool that looked better than those."

"I'm taking a class from Chad," I said.

"Learnin' to make globs?"

"We haven't gotten that far yet. But I'm not blown away by his work, either," I admitted.

"They'd make good weights for lobster pots," he mused. "Might scare off the lobsters, though."

"Oh, they're not that bad!"

He gave me a look.

"Well, maybe they are."

"Mmm," he said. "Well, they're somethin'." As he spoke, there was the sound of a door opening. A moment later, Claudette's weak voice drifted over from the house. "Eli?"

He just about dropped the sander and sprinted toward the house. "I'm comin', sweetheart! What's wrong?"

"I got a bad feeling about Muffin and Pudge," she said. Her two goats were the apples of her eye, even if they were the bane of the local gardeners' existence. "Can you go check on them?"

Eli looked at me.

"Where are they?" I asked him.

"Down in the meadow before Blueberry Hill," he said.

"On my way home, then," I said.

"Ayuh." He nodded.

"I'll check on them and move them if I need to," I said. "Let me know about Claudette, okay? No matter what the news is."

"I will," he said, brushing sawdust off his flannel shirt. "I'm going to go check on Claudie. Thanks for lookin' in on the goats."

"Anytime," I said. "I mean it."

16

*M*uffin and Pudge were, in fact, on Blueberry Hill, and it was a good thing I went to check on them. The goats, being intelligent creatures, had learned how to work in tandem to relocate the tire that served as their anchor.

Today, I could track their progress across the field. A zigzag strip of denuded meadow lay behind the goats, who had munched their way over the hill and were now making a beeline for my friend Emmeline's prize petunias.

I hurried ahead of them to Emmeline's door and knocked. She answered almost immediately, and as she opened the door, the front porch filled with the delicious smell of baking. Her sharp eyes were merry. "Natalie! How are you? Nice of you to visit... I was just about to pull a cake out of the oven."

"Sorry to interrupt," I said, noting the potholders on her hands, "but Muffin and Pudge have scented your petunias, and if we don't do something fast, you're going to have bare window boxes."

"Oh, dear," Emmeline said, pursing her lips and looking

past me to the two goats, who were straining at their chains and moving the tire an inch at a time. "I love Claudette, but her goats are a menace. What do we do?"

"If the boxes are mobile, I'd move them out of harm's way," I suggested. "I can move the goats, but as you can tell, they are more than capable of moving themselves."

Emmeline sighed. "Claudette just doesn't seem to be out taking care of them as much lately. In fact, I haven't seen her much at all."

"I think she may be under the weather," I said vaguely.

Emmeline, as usual, missed nothing. "What do you mean, under the weather?" she asked, her bright, birdlike eyes fixing on me. "Do you know something?"

"No," I lied. "I just haven't seen her as much, and Eli says she's been resting more lately."

"Hmph," she said, clearly not believing me. "Well, I can tell you're not going to spill the beans, so I'm going to have to bring over some cake this evening and pry it out of her. In the meantime, let me get the cake out of the oven and then we'll move those boxes before the goats turn them into dessert."

"I'll get the first one," I volunteered. "Where do you want them?"

"The sunporch in the back should work for now," she said. "Unless you think they'll break through the glass to get them."

"I don't think so, but with Muffin and Pudge, you never know."

"We'll have to risk it," she said.

"I'll get started," I said. As she went back in to contend with her cake, I lifted the first box and walked around the house to the sunporch, the goats eyeing me with interest. "This isn't for you," I informed them. By the time I'd gotten

both boxes back to the sunporch, the goats had lost interest
and were pulling back toward a tasty patch of grass in the
meadow, and Emmeline had taken her cake out of the oven.

"Come on in," she said.

"Are you sure?"

"Of course. You can have a piece of cake with me.
Consider it a reward for saving my petunias."

"Thanks," I said, following her into her cozy kitchen. A
half-finished afghan in shades of purple sat on a chair, knitting needles protruding from it, and a variety of teapots and
teacups festooned the windowsill.

"What kind of cake?" I asked, practically drooling from
the sweet smell.

"Sour cream coffee cake," she said. "It was my mother's
favorite cake."

"If it tastes anything like it smells, I can see why," I said.

"I'll turn it out of the pan in a minute and we can both
have a slice," she said. "In the meantime, you can tell me all
about what's going on out at the inn. I hear you've had some
excitement."

"More than I like, unfortunately," I said. As she bustled
with the tea things and we waited for the cake to cool, I
filled her in on everything that had happened.

"Do you think what happened to that young woman was
linked to what's going on down at the co-op?"

"It's possible," I said. "Someone cut loose all the boats the
morning she died. What are the odds that that was a coincidence?"

"True," she said.

On the other hand, Chelsea had known Bruce and
Noelle... and they both had a motive for wanting Chelsea
out of the way. And then there was Chad. There was obviously no love lost between Chad and Chelsea, although I

didn't know why, but a motive for murder? The antipathy I'd seen was hardly enough to warrant murder. I briefly considered Quartz as a possibility... what if she considered Chelsea a threat? But as far as I knew, she hadn't met Chelsea. Unless Chelsea had gone to Chad's room the night she arrived and discovered Quartz there? But Chelsea had seemed surprised to see Chad that morning.

And then there was whoever had left that cat on my doorstep. Was it connected to Chelsea's murder? Did someone not want me looking into her death or into the lobster fishery?

I felt like I was jousting at windmills.

"This may seem like a weird question, but have you heard any rumors about Mac and Earl being up to something?" I asked Emmeline.

"I know Mac's sister came in from Northeast Harbor and was at his place last week," she said, and leaned in. "Just between you and me, I heard she was trying to get him into rehab."

"Rehab? For alcohol?"

She shook her head. "He hurt his back a few years ago," she said. "Got hooked on painkillers, from what I hear. I'm not sure if he's moved on to something else or not, but she's worried about him."

"That sounds bad," I said.

"It does," she agreed. "He and Earl were friends for a long time... grew up together. It's gotten bad the last year or two, though. I don't know if it's because of the pain meds, or what."

"Mac rammed Earl's boat," I said.

"I know," she told me. "I'm wondering if it had something to do with Mac's sister's being in town. Maybe she talked to Earl, tried to get him to help, and Mac got mad."

"I heard it was because Mac thought Earl called in the fisheries inspector."

"That could be the party line," she suggested with a shrug. "He's not about to tell the world his friend wanted him in rehab, is he?"

"No, probably not," I said. "Apparently, Mac said something to Earl about a 'snow day.' Is that some kind of island or lobster slang I don't know about?"

She shook her head. "If it is, I've never heard of it. And I've lived here my whole life."

I sighed.

The teakettle began to whistle. She busied herself making tea in a teapot shaped like a cabbage, filling a small pitcher with milk and setting it on the table with two cups and a bowl of sugar, then turned to the cake. "Now. I think this is about ready to turn out of the pan." As I watched, she slipped a knife between the cake and the pan and eased it around to make sure the cake wouldn't stick. Then she put a baking rack under the Bundt pan and inverted it, giving it a few good taps. When she lifted the pan, a beautiful golden cake stood on the cooling rack. I could see the streusel middle of nuts and brown sugar, and my mouth started to water.

"I'll just whip up the glaze and finish it off and we'll try it," she said. "I saw the *Daily Mail*," she said nonchalantly as she measured confectioners' sugar into a bowl. "Are Gwen and Adam still speaking with you?"

"Gwen is," I said. "But she's not happy."

"I can't believe you told Gertrude that," she said.

"She overheard a conversation," I told her. "She drew conclusions."

"Looks pretty bad, if you ask me. We need to find out what really happened, and fast."

"I know." I grimaced.

She mixed in milk with the sugar and a touch of vanilla extract, then began glazing the cake. I was dying for a piece of it, particularly now, considering the topic of conversation. "And you still won't tell me what's going on with Claudette?"

"I just know she's tired," I said. "I think she's going to get checked out, but that's all I know."

"Well, then," she said. "I'm going down there tonight to find out."

"Let me know if you hear anything," I said.

"Maybe I will, and maybe I won't," she said, finishing the glaze and cutting two big pieces. "In the meantime, have a piece of cake. You look like you need it."

I really, really did.

I LEFT Emmeline's stuffed with sour cream coffee cake and tea, and grateful for friends who were generous and knew how to bake. I was still worried, though. As I walked down the hill toward the inn, Quartz appeared, wearing skin-tight leggings, heavy eye makeup, and a spandex top that left little to the imagination. The crystals hanging around her neck flashed in the sunlight as she walked.

"Hey," she said. "You're the innkeeper, right? You're taking the pottery class?"

"I am," I said.

"Chad is just amazing, isn't he?" she gushed, eyes sparkling. "I mean, the way he expresses himself... it's so, like... amorphous, almost."

"Amorphous. Good word," I said.

"Anyway, I just stopped by to say hi, but his room was

being cleaned and it looks like all his stuff is gone. Do you know where he went?"

"I think he moved to a house on the island," I told her. "His parents arrived this morning and checked him out during breakfast."

"They did?" She rolled her eyes. "He must be so pissed at them. They're always putting their noses in where they don't belong. I mean, their son is an accomplished artist. He doesn't need their interference."

"I thought they were funding the Art Guild?"

"It's family money," she said. "They just did it as a philanthropic thing. It's a tax write-off."

"Well, his parents paid his bill," I said, hoping she'd understand what she was getting herself into with Chad, regardless of what he'd been telling her about philanthropy and tax write-offs. "I think they rented his new place for him, too. From what I can tell, he's not paying for much."

"It's going to be his one day anyway," she said. "His parents pay for as much as they can because of the inheritance tax. He could do it himself, of course, but they just work the funding this way to minimize taxes."

"Huh," I said, not convinced. From what I could see, Chad hadn't actually worked a day in his life. I guess if you were expecting to inherit millions, why would you? Although I probably would.

"His dad was so pissed that that chick from college was on the island."

"What?"

"That Chelsea girl. The one who got herself killed."

17

"*H*ow did Chad's dad know her?"

"She was on the newspaper at Middlesex, where they went to school. She wrote a whole article on how Chad's dad bought Chad's way into the school by funding part of a building. It was all bull, of course, but the local papers picked it up."

"Did he?"

Quartz fiddled with one of her crystals. "Did he what?"

"Buy part of a building."

"He paid to build a new art studio," she said. "But that's totally not why Chad got in. You can see how talented he is."

"Right," I said. "When did he find out Chelsea was here?"

"The night she arrived. His dad came by. He was visiting Chad, and they walked out into the hall, and there she was."

"I didn't see anyone who wasn't a guest that night," I said.

"I don't think he stayed long. But he was mad about Chelsea. He was convinced she was on the island under-cover to write another thing on Chad."

"But she was a fisheries observer!"

"Chad's dad didn't believe that. He thought she was here as an undercover reporter."

"Why? Why would she come here to report on Chad?" From what I could see, he wasn't exactly burning up the art scene.

"Chad's dad is always obsessed with reputation," she said. "His wife's some kind of socialite from New York. His dad kind of worked his way up in the real estate business, but she was a blue blood, from what Chad told me."

"You know a lot about Chad's family."

"We've been dating for the last few months," she said. "He was talking about doing a mermaid statue of me. He hasn't said the L-word yet, but I think it's only a matter of time." She straightened a little, and her eyes sparkled. "I've been trying to decide what kind of ring I want."

Whoa. She was thinking about rings already? I thought about what I'd overheard Chad telling someone on the phone at the Guild. I would bet my bottom dollar Chad didn't see Quartz in the same way she saw him, and my heart ached to think of her future disappointment. "I'm sure a mermaid statue would be... lovely," I said. If his sea creatures looked like they'd been run over by trucks, I could only imagine what Chad would do if he attempted a human-type form, but I didn't share my thoughts. "But as for the long-term... you're still so young. Are you sure you want to settle down yet?"

"I'm twenty-two!" she said, as if she were approaching Social Security age. "I wasn't sure I was ready, and then I met Chad," she continued. "He bought me this crystal." She proffered a clear crystal on a black cord. "Quartz. Just like my name."

"Pretty," I said. "Do you get along with his parents?"

She shrugged. "I haven't spent a lot of time with them. I only met his dad."

"You said he was on the island the night before we found Chelsea. How did he get here?"

"I think he took a water taxi," she said. "I asked about the yacht—Chad had told me about it—but he said their captain had the night off, so he left it on the mainland. I think he was a little surprised to see me."

"Why was he here?"

"He said he was planning on taking Chad to dinner, but you know how this island is. Not a lot of restaurants."

"By the way, did you stay over that night? I think I found your barrette in his room."

She blinked. "What? No," she said. "I don't think I'm missing a barrette." She fiddled with the crystal nervously, then clasped it in her hand, as if she were afraid to lose it. "What did it look like?"

"It was a butterfly," I said. "It had crystals on it, so I thought it might be yours."

"No," she repeated. "I don't have anything like that."

I shrugged. "Maybe it was there from another guest and I missed it during the cleaning," I suggested, although I was pretty sure the clip was connected to Quartz somehow. "Or maybe he was planning to give it to you. Who knows?"

"Yeah," she said, but she sounded unconvinced. "You're right. Maybe he just hadn't given it to me yet."

"Who knows?" I repeated.

She pursed her lips, still clutching the crystal. "You don't know where he's staying?"

"Sorry," I said. "I don't."

"He didn't text me," she said. "Maybe the reception's bad."

"It's on and off here on the island," I admitted. "You could try him at the Guild," I suggested.

"He wasn't there earlier."

"I'm sure he'll turn up," I said.

"I'm sure," she said, but with much less confidence than she had had a few minutes before.

"Before you go," I said, "do you know when Chad's parents left the island?"

"I think they went back that night, but I don't know; I ended up going back to my place."

"If you find out, let me know," I said.

"I will. Anyway, I guess I'll go back to the Art Guild. If you see him, will you tell him to call or text?"

"Of course," I said.

"Thanks. See you!" she said, and headed down the road, still clutching her crystals and looking a lot less carefree than when I'd encountered her.

I hoped Chad didn't break her heart too badly. And that if he did, her heart healed quickly.

ON THE WAY back to the inn, I decided to detour to the Cranberry Island store, in part to check in with Charlene and in part to pick up sour cream for the stroganoff I was planning to make for dinner.

"You're still alive," she said as I walked through the door. Charlene was restocking the chicken broth from a box, and was the most put-together stock clerk I'd ever seen. Today, she wore charcoal eyeliner that matched her sparkly gray V-neck and flared jeans that hugged her curvy form. I could see why my cousin—and most of the men on the island—were smitten.

"I am still alive," I confirmed. "At least for now."

"I thought Adam might skewer you. Or Gwen."

I winced. "Any news?"

"Well, Adam was in earlier, and once he saw the paper, he was furious," she said. "Gwen came in a few minutes later and talked him down, but he was livid. I told him I'd heard you leave a message for Gertrude saying you really didn't have anything to say, but I don't think he bought it."

"I'll bet not, based on what's in the paper," I said. I had some work to do to win back Gwen's trust—and Adam's. I hoped finding out what had really happened to Chelsea might help. "Have you heard anything that might possibly be related to what happened to the fisheries observer?"

"Nothing yet," she said. "You?"

"Well, everyone here seems to think she was undercover, but no one can agree on what." I relayed what Quartz had told me about Chad and Chelsea's history... and shared what I now knew about Bruce and Noelle.

"So Chad's dad thought she was here for a scoop on Chad."

"It doesn't make sense, but apparently, he was livid," I said. "I wish I knew if he was here the morning she died."

"I didn't see his yacht."

"He got here some other way. Water taxi, maybe?"

"I could call the guy who runs the taxi to see if he remembers him," Charlene volunteered.

"That would be great," I said.

"Do you think the married folks might be responsible?"

"Is someone finding out about your affair a motive for murder?" I asked.

She shrugged. "Depends on what's at stake."

"You're right," I agreed. "I need to look in to the two of

them some more. I glanced at their Facebook profiles, but I don't know anything more about them."

"Let me know," she said.

"And poor Quartz is going to have her heart broken, I'm afraid."

"The one who walks around with all those crystals bumping on her chest?"

"Yes, that one," I said. "She's set her sights on Chad, but I think she's just the flavor of the month for him. Maybe even the week."

"Been there, done that," she said.

"But not with Robert," I said quickly. "Speaking of Robert, how's that going?"

"Oh, Natalie, you should have introduced us years ago!" she said. "He had a work emergency so he had to go back to Bangor, but he's planning a weekend getaway to Nova Scotia soon."

"I'm glad things are going well for someone," I said.

"It's a nice change of pace," she agreed. "I just hope I don't find out he's a werewolf or something."

"I don't remember any full-moon transformations growing up," I said, "so I think you're good. But back to Adam... any word on his boat?"

She shook her head. "None," she told me. "Talk about a bad week. First the paper... oh." She covered her mouth with one hand, eyes wide. "Sorry!"

"It's okay. It's my fault, after all. Any ideas on where the boat might be?"

"I think they're afraid it sank," she said.

"He's got insurance, though, right?"

"He does, but it'll take weeks to get it sorted out, and then he's got to get a new boat, new gear..." She shook her head. "He'll lose a lot of income. And he and Gwen were saving for a house; it may have to wait."

"Gwen mentioned that," I said. As I spoke, the bell at the front door jingled, and Tom Lockhart walked in, a frown on his weathered face.

"Any news on the *Carpe Diem*?" I asked as the lanky lobsterman strode across the store floor.

"None yet," he said. "I just hope she didn't go down."

"Me too," I said. "Any thoughts on who might have cut all the mooring lines?"

"We're investigating still," he said.

"That's what Lorraine told me," I said. "Hey... what do you know about Earl Randall and Mac Penney?"

"They've been friends and rivals for years," Tom said in a guarded tone. "I think Mac may have had one too many PBRs the night of their run-in."

"I understand Mac might have had troubles beyond beer," I said.

He narrowed his eyes. "What? Who told you that?"

"I don't remember," I said, remembering my promise to Josie. "It was just a rumor."

"I'd appreciate it if you didn't repeat it," he said shortly. "Rumors cause trouble."

"I understand that," I said. "But one of my guests died recently. I think Mac thought she was undercover with the Marine Patrol. If he had something to hide, the police need to know about it."

"I thought John was the deputy," Tom replied, his voice tense.

"He is," I said. "But I'd like to find out who the murderer is so that I know it's safe to sleep at the inn."

"And so you can get Adam off the hot seat, too, I presume. I went by his place a few minutes ago. One of those detectives was there; they must have seen the article, too."

"Who didn't see the article?" I groaned.

"Why did you tell Gertrude about our business?" he asked, looking more unfriendly than I'd ever seen him.

"I didn't," I protested. "I called her and left a brief message, and my phone must not have hung up. I think she recorded a conversation that took place in the store."

Tom did not look at all appeased. "But you said those things."

"We were just talking about what folks were saying on the island," Charlene interjected. "Neither of us think Adam had anything to do with it, obviously."

"See what I mean about repeating rumors?" Tom said. "They're dangerous."

Charlene and I exchanged glances.

"Anyway, I'm just here for my mail," he said.

"Got it," Charlene said, opening his box and fishing out a stack of letters. The top one was marked FINAL NOTICE; the sender was a mortgage company. Tom noticed me looking and shielded the envelope from view.

"Thanks," he said to Charlene, then nodded to both of us and strode out of the store.

"What was that all about?" Charlene asked me when the door shut, the bell jangling. "I've never seen him so surly."

"He sure isn't happy about all the scandal on the island," I said. "And did you take a look at his mail? That top envelope looked like a nastygram from a mortgage company to me."

"Tania sorted the mail today; I didn't look at it."

"I hate to suggest this, but if Tom's having financial problems, do you think maybe he had something to do with what happened to Chelsea?"

"Why would he?"

"If he knew there was something going on that shouldn't be... if the co-op goes down, his income does, too."

"If that's the case, then it wouldn't make sense for him to be the person who cut all the boats free."

"Unless he wanted to cover his tracks," I said. "All the lobstermen are usually out fishing in the morning, which would mean they'd all have alibis. If no one's out on the water, though, everyone's a suspect."

"Still, it's not good for co-op revenues," Charlene said. "Besides, I can't see Tom doing that."

"Usually I'd agree, but there's something fishy about him lately."

"Tom? A murderer?" Charlene waved away the idea. "Natalie, I'm beginning to think you're desperate to pin this murder on someone."

I was about to answer when my phone rang.

"Hello?"

"Oh, thank God." It was John.

"What do you mean?"

"You're okay."

"So far," I said. "What's wrong?"

"Someone attacked Quartz."

18

"Oh, no," I breathed. "I just talked to her this afternoon. How bad is she?"

"I'm with her now; Catherine found her, just down the way from the Art Guild, in the trees off Seal Point Road. The paramedics and the mainland police are on their way. She's unconscious, and looks like she's lost a lot of blood."

"Poor thing," I said. "What happened?"

"Blunt force trauma to the head," he said shortly.

I gripped the phone harder. "Just like Chelsea."

"Just like Chelsea."

"I'm coming over," I said.

"I'd rather you not."

"I want to be with you," I said. "I'll tell Charlene where I'm going. And I'll grab a pair of scissors if it makes you feel better."

"I don't want you to come alone," he said. "It's not safe."

"I'll see if I can get someone to come with me," I promised.

"You'd better," he said. "I don't want to lose you."

"You won't," I promised. I hung up the phone and turned to Charlene, who was staring at me wide-eyed.

"Someone attacked that young woman, Quartz. Same way as Chelsea."

Charlene paled. "Is she alive?"

"For now," I told her. "Paramedics are on the way."

"This is freaking me out," she said. "I need to call Tania, make sure she's okay. Both those young women..."

Could it be someone targeting young women? I wondered as Charlene reached for the phone. "I'm going to be with them until the paramedics get there; Catherine found her close to the Art Guild on Seal Point Road."

"Is it safe?"

"Whoever it is isn't using a gun, at least," I said. "I want to go be with them, but I need to find someone to go with me."

"I'll go," she volunteered.

"What about the store?"

She walked to the front door and flipped the OPEN sign to CLOSED. "People can wait. Let's go."

QUARTZ WAS a little way off the road, in a clump of blueberry bushes. The crystals around her neck still sparkled in the sunlight, but Quartz's eyes were closed. Her sprawled, unconscious body reminded me of Chelsea's. I shivered, hoping Quartz wouldn't meet the same end.

Charlene was still on the phone with Tania, exhorting her to stay in her house and lock the door for the time being. Catherine stood a few feet away, a grim look on her face, and John crouched at Quartz's head. He had stripped down to an undershirt and was holding his button-down flannel shirt against the wound, which appeared to be on the back of her head. The green-and-blue-plaid fabric was stained dark red, and there was a coppery scent in the air.

"How's her breathing?" I asked.

"Steady so far," he said. "I'm trying to keep her from bleeding too much, but it's still coming."

As he spoke, Quartz murmured something.

I held up a hand and crouched beside her. "What, Quartz?"

"Cha..."

I glanced up at John, then back at Quartz.

"Chad? Did Chad do this to you?"

"Chad," she murmured, tossing her head from side to side.

"Don't move," John said gently. "You're hurt."

"Not good 'nough," she slurred.

"Not good enough?" I asked. "Who's not good enough?"

She opened her eyes wide for a moment, and then her head rolled to the side again.

"Quartz? Quartz?" I put my hand on her chest; it was moving, but only slightly. "The paramedics had better get here soon," I said. "I'm afraid we're going to lose her."

"What was she talking about?" Quinn asked.

"Something about Chad," Catherine said. "It almost seemed like she was saying he wasn't good enough. Or she wasn't."

"So Chad hit her over the head?" I asked. "If he wanted to end things, wouldn't it be easier to just break up?"

"Maybe she was a bit upset about the breakup. Maybe what happened was an accident," Catherine suggested.

"If Chelsea hadn't died of a similar wound, I might be willing to entertain that theory," I said, "but it's too similar. Hit over the head, right near a road or path..."

"Chad knew Chelsea, too," John pointed out.

"That's true," I said. "I was assuming what happened to Chelsea was linked to the lobster co-op, though. I mean, why else cut all the boats free unless you were trying to cover your tracks?"

"It's a fair point," Charlene said.

"Plus," I said, "I keep hearing rumors that Chelsea was undercover. She used to be a reporter at Middlesex, so there's talk she might be a journalist on assignment."

"Reporting on what?" Catherine asked.

"Maybe whatever's going on down at the co-op," I suggested.

"Half the co-op thought she was a Marine Patrol officer," Charlene said, and turned to John. "Have you heard anything?"

"The mainland police are being rather tight-lipped. Probably because of that article in the paper this morning."

I winced again. "If I could have a take-back..."

"Mistakes happen to all of us," John said. "I'm sure it will come right."

"I hope so," I said, looking down at Quartz's prone form. There was something clutched in her right hand, and it wasn't a crystal.

"There's money in her hand," I said.

"There is," Charlene said, squatting down to peer at it. It was partially covered with last year's dead leaves; she blew them out of the way to look at the denomination. "A lot of it, too. The top one is a hundred, and there's a stack of bills."

"Did Chad give her money to go away?" I asked. "If he did, why not take it back after he hit her?" And did he kill Chelsea before she could humiliate him a second time? I wondered. I'd heard of narcissism before, but from what I knew of him, a double murder seemed rather extreme.

Then again, I didn't know him very well.

"Maybe he panicked in the heat of the moment?" Charlene said. "I don't know. It does seem weird to just leave it."

"This whole thing doesn't add up," John said. "The altercation between Mac and Earl. The mooring lines cut in the harbor. Chelsea, who'd just come to the island the night before she died. If this was just a lovers' quarrel, how do you explain the rest of it?"

"I found a barrette in Chad's room the other morning," I said, still watching Quartz. Her breathing was shallow but steady. I hoped the paramedics would get here soon.

"A barrette?" Charlene asked, puzzled. "What about it? Maybe he likes wearing his hair up."

"I don't see how you'd fit dreads into a barrette, and I don't think he's the crystal butterfly type. I thought it was Quartz's, but it wasn't. I told her about it just this afternoon."

"Ohhh... I see. You're thinking she confronted him, and things got nasty," Charlene suggested.

"It's possible. I don't think he was too hung up on her, though, so I can't see a breakup being a big issue for him. I'm wondering if maybe she knew something about him she threatened to expose if he didn't give up his other girlfriend, whoever she is. Assuming there was one."

"A big assumption based on one barrette," John reminded me.

"I'm brainstorming here."

"Maybe she told him he wasn't good enough to be an artist, and he went berserk or something," Charlene theorized.

"And hit her over the head with a rock? Was he seeing Chelsea, then, too, and did the same thing happen with her?" Catherine asked.

I shook my head. "Like I said, I don't think he'd be too torn up about losing Quartz. And I don't think he and

Chelsea were an item. But I do think he was still irked over the article she wrote about him in college."

"What did the article say that was so bad?" Catherine asked.

"It pretty much said his parents bought his way into Middlesex College," I said.

"That's got to have been mortifying for him," John said, readjusting the shirt under Quartz's head gently as he spoke. "Still, though, they're what... twenty-five? Why not kill her when the article came out? Why wait?"

"Maybe he thought she was going to do a further exposé," I said. "Maybe revealing that his parents paid for him to be part of the Art Guild, essentially."

"Which they did, from what I hear," Catherine said. "His pottery is... well, disappointing."

"It is," I said, agreeing with her. "But it still doesn't explain all the other things going on." Including Tom Lockhart's edginess at the store today.

"Everything's all wrong on the island lately," John's mother said, her arms crossed over her chest and her blue eyes misty. I knew she was thinking not just of Quartz and Chelsea, but of Murray and Sarah. "I'd like it to get back to normal."

"You and me both," I said, looking down at Quartz and praying that she'd be okay.

19

By the time the paramedics and the police had come and gone, it was almost time for dinner. I didn't have a full house tonight; only four guests, Emma, Thuy, Bruce, and Noelle, would be at the inn, but I still needed to put something on the table. I didn't know where Sarah was, but odds were good Murray would be wining and dining her.

Catherine thought so, too, and voiced the opinion several times as we walked Charlene home and then headed back to the inn together. John was going to swing by the Art Guild again to talk to Thuy before following us back to the inn.

As we neared the top of the hill before the road curved down toward the inn, voices reached our ears.

"That's it. I'm going home."

"But Noelle!"

Catherine and I glanced at each other. Then, without a word, we both detoured off the road and crouched down in the bushes as Noelle appeared at the top of the hill, her rolling suitcase and Bruce trailing behind her.

"I think you killed that girl," she said. Her heart-shaped face was white; she looked angry and frightened. "I think you don't want your wife to find out about us. You say we're going to be together someday, but I think you're lying."

"I would never do something like that!" he said. "I tried to talk to her, but that's all."

"You were yelling at her... you threatened her. I heard you. And you didn't come back to the room." She was crying now. "And then that other girl overheard us, too. What are you going to do, kill her, too?"

"Noelle," he said. "I would never do something like that. Never. I'm begging you, please. Don't go."

"I am going to go," she announced, starting back down the road. "And I'm going to tell Frank all about us before he hears about it from somewhere (or someone?) else. And then we're going to go to counseling and see if we can put things back together."

"But you won't tell Delilah, will you?" Bruce's voice was syrupy sweet. Noelle stopped short and turned to face him.

"Really? After all the things you said to me, about how we were going to have a life together, about how I was the only woman for you, about how you never felt this way with anyone else..." Tears formed in her eyes. "You're more worried about keeping Delilah than about keeping me."

"It's the kids," he said weakly. "Darling. You know you're the only one for me. We're just victims of circumstance..."

"No," she said. "It's not the kids. It's Delilah's paycheck, and that big, two-story house, isn't it?" She narrowed her reddened eyes at him. "Well, you're going to be in bad shape soon. She's the best divorce attorney in Portland. She's going to take you to the cleaners."

"And what about you?" he demanded, his handsome face red now. "You're not exactly innocent either. What are you going to do when I tell Frank about everything that happened between us? And I mean *everything*."

She took a deep breath. "It'll kill him, but I don't know what else to do," she said, "I can't live this way anymore. I can't live a lie. I thought I knew you, but you're... you're someone else."

"Noelle," he said, his voice suddenly calm in a very disturbing way. The hackles rose on the back of my neck. Noelle felt it, too; she yanked her roller bag and started walking down the hill, almost jogging.

"You're not going anywhere," he said, lurching after her and grabbing her arm.

"Leave me alone," she hissed, jerking her arm away. The sleeve of her pink sweater tore. He grabbed her wrist hard, twisting it so she was forced to turn toward him.

"I can't let you leave here," he told her in a silky voice. "I can't let you destroy my family."

"You should have thought about that six months ago," she spat, her hair mussed. There was still anger in her face, but I could read more fear now. "Let me go."

"No," he said, back to cajoling. "Come back to the inn. Let's talk about it. We can end things if you want, but why bring up trouble when we don't have to? If you tell Frank and Delilah, you'll only be hurting yourself and your children."

She sagged a little, considering it. He sensed her weakness and moved in, caressing her hair. Her eyes fluttered a bit, and she leaned into him.

"That's my girl," he said in a satisfied tone. "I knew you'd see reason."

As he spoke, she seemed to snap out of a trance. "It's all just words, Bruce," she said, swiping at her eyes. "I thought I loved you. I did. But now I see..."

"See what?"

"This is all a game for you," she said. "But I'm not playing anymore."

"I won't let you leave," he said. "I'll kill you before I let you leave."

"You wouldn't," she said in a feeble voice.

"Do you want to try me? Come here," he ordered.

"No. Bruce..."

He caught up with her in two steps and grabbed her by the throat. Her hands flailed, and the roller bag bumped down the hill.

"No," she said in a breathy voice. "No..."

I glanced at Catherine. Together, we stood up and stepped out of the bushes.

"Stop!" I yelled. "Let her go."

Bruce's hand dropped. "We were just talking," he said quickly.

"We heard," Catherine said. "Before you get any handsier," she admonished Bruce, "my son is a deputy."

"And there are plenty more police on the island," I added.

"What? Why?" Noelle asked.

"Someone attacked Quartz," I said.

Noelle looked at Bruce with wide eyes, and her hand drifted to her throat. "You *did* try to kill her. And you killed that other girl, too. Chelsea. You're sick."

"No," he said. "Noelle, no. I'd never do that."

"You just tried to strangle me," she said in a small, stunned voice. "You're a murderer."

"No," he said. "You've got it all wrong."

"Why don't you come with us?" I suggested. "We can wait down at the inn."

"No," he said, looking around wildly. He ran a hand

through his hair, and then, suddenly, turned and bolted in the direction of the inn.

Noelle looked at us. "Where's he going?"

"I don't know," I said. "But you're safe now."

She crumpled to the ground, and I ran to support her. "I thought I was in love with a murderer," she said.

"I'm so sorry," I told her.

"My life is ruined," she murmured. "All ruined." As she spoke, there was the whine of a motor. I looked down toward the dock in time to see John's skiff, *Mooncatcher*, roaring toward the mainland.

"He's gone," I said, and looked up at Catherine, who was watching the skiff recede into the distance with a grim look on her face.

"I'll call the harbormaster at Northeast Harbor," Catherine said, pulling out her phone and walking down the hill to retrieve the lost rolling bag as I helped Noelle back to the inn.

"I feel so stupid," Noelle said as she picked at a scone in my warm yellow kitchen. Smudge, sensing her upset, had jumped up into her lap, and Biscuit was weaving around her ankles. Catherine had come into the kitchen after us, pulling Noelle's bag behind her, and then excused herself, sensing that two people might be one too many for Noelle right now.

"It happens," I told her. "I admire you for wanting to put an end to things and be honest."

"It's going to ruin my marriage, probably."

"Maybe," I said. "Maybe not."

"I tried so hard to put him off," she said, "but the more I objected, the more he pushed. I should have been stronger."

"You can't change the past," I said gently as I filled the teakettle and put it on the stove. "If you were vulnerable, it sounds like there might have been some trouble in the marriage to start with. I think it's fairly common to grow apart a bit when kids get thrown into the mix." I turned on the burner and sat down across from her. "Do you still love your husband?"

"I do," she said. "I can't believe I did this to him."

"I'm so sorry," I said.

"And Bruce... to think he killed that girl Chelsea." She looked up at me. "Will the other girl be okay? Crystal?"

"Quartz," I said. "I don't know yet, but they've taken her to the hospital. Why do you think he killed her?"

"She heard us talking," she said. "We were arguing on the back porch, and she just... appeared. I told Bruce not to worry, but he was convinced she'd heard something, and raced off to talk to her."

"She didn't say anything about it when I saw her," I said.

"When did you see her?"

"A little while before she was found," I told her.

"He did come back," she said. "Said he'd convinced her it was a misunderstanding."

I thought about the money in Quartz's hand. "Out of curiosity, did he usually carry a lot of cash?"

She blinked. "How did you know? He did everything in cash so there wouldn't be a paper trail."

"Just curious," I said. "What happened with Chelsea?"

"We both panicked when we saw her in the dining room," she told me. "She lived in our neighborhood; I saw her when I was walking my dog, and she knew my husband."

"Small world," I said.

"Too small. Anyway, I couldn't eat another bite once I saw her. We went back to our room and tried to figure out what to do." She pushed her hair behind her ears, still looking anxious. "He saw her leaving the inn and went to talk to her. He came back a few minutes later and told me she'd said she wasn't going to say anything."

"How long was he gone?" I asked.

"About twenty minutes, I guess. I took a shower while he was gone, to clear my head; when I got out, he was back in the room. And now I know... oh, God. I can't believe it." She buried her head in her hands.

I reached out to touch her shoulder. "It's been a pretty horrible weekend for you, hasn't it?" I asked.

She wiped her eyes and looked up at me. "Not as bad for me as it was for those poor girls. What do I tell Delilah? She's got to know she's married to a murderer."

"I think you should let the police worry about that," I said.

We sat in silence for a few minutes, waiting for the kettle to boil. All this time I'd thought Chelsea's death had had something to do with the lobster co-op, or maybe Chad... and it had been Bruce who'd done it.

Who had cut the mooring lines of the lobster boats, though? Why had someone left that stuffed cat on my front doorstep, and made the anonymous call? What was going on between Mac and Earl? And what had Quartz been talking about when she talked about Chad, and being enough?

It seemed as if we'd found the murderer, but things still weren't adding up.

I looked at Noelle, mascara streaks on her pale cheeks and her big eyes haunted, trying to imagine how she must feel. She'd jeopardized her whole life for a man who was mentally unstable and violent. How was she going to pick up the pieces and move on?

There was no way to be sure, but I did know one thing. For all her mistakes, Noelle was a strong woman... and a moral one. She'd been willing to admit her mistakes and do the right thing.

I just hoped she'd be able to recover.

"So it was Bruce all along," Charlene said when she and John got back to the inn a half hour later, one of the detectives with them. The detective had escorted Noelle to the dining room to take a statement, and the rest of us were sitting in the kitchen.

"I guess so," I said. "But it feels... wrong somehow."

"Wrong?" Charlene asked.

"Yeah," I said. "It's like I'm missing something."

"I know what you mean," John said. "Maybe there are just two things going on, and we're kind of mixing them up."

"Maybe," I said. But I still wasn't convinced.

20

"*A*re you still up for that art class this afternoon?" Catherine asked the next morning as I finished cleaning up the breakfast dishes.

"Why not?" I asked, drying my hands on a towel and then hanging it on the oven door. "I'd like to go early to see if I can smooth things over with Gwen."

"Sure," she said. "Any word on that poor girl?"

"Stable but still unconscious, from what I've heard," I told her. "I hope she comes out of it."

"Me too," Catherine said.

I looked at John's mother closely. Her hair was freshly styled, she was wearing pearl earrings, and she had on a cashmere sweater that was the exact color of her eyes. "You seem better today."

"I am," she said. "I was thinking about it last night. There were a lot of things about Murray that bothered me. If he's willing to throw me over just for the chance to date someone new on the island, maybe he's not the kind of man I want to be out with anyway."

"That sounds positive," I said.

"Besides," she said, "I don't see myself with a man who favors brass bathroom fixtures."

I grinned. "We have to have standards. I'm glad you're feeling better about it."

"Thanks, Natalie," she said. "I mean, I still want Sarah to fall off a cliff or something, don't get me wrong. And if she took Murray with her, I wouldn't object."

"I've been there myself," I said. "I totally get it."

"But instead of coming up with exciting ways to murder them, I think I'm going to talk to Charlene about online dating."

"That sounds like a great idea." I was impressed. I'd been a mess for months when I'd been dumped for another woman many years ago. "Let me know what I can do to help."

"I will," she said and looked down at herself. "You know, I kind of forgot we were working with clay when I got dressed this morning. I think I'm going to go change into something more casual."

"You look great, but that's probably a good call," I said. "I'll just send off that scone recipe and we'll go, okay?"

"Sounds like a plan," she said.

I went to the office and submitted both scone recipes— the limit was two—along with a short e-mail telling the contest administrator about the inn. I had just hit Send when my phone rang.

"Good morning, Gray Whale Inn."

It was Charlene. "They found Adam's boat."

"Oh, thank goodness. Is it okay?"

"She got a little banged up, but it should be an easy fix."

I leaned back in my chair, looking out the back windows of the inn at the blue water and the green-gray humps of Mount Desert Island in the distance. "Where was she?"

"Headed out to sea," she said. "She was spotted by a lobsterman from Southwest Harbor. He called it in, and they're towing her now."

So the *Carpe Diem* hadn't sunk to the bottom of the ocean. "What a relief."

"I know. He was in here just a few minutes ago, in high spirits. I think you're forgiven for your oversight."

I sat up straight in my chair. "Really?"

"Really. There was an article in this morning's paper; they found Bruce on Route 3 and arrested him last night. Gertrude got the scoop and published the story. They're charging him with murder."

"Oh," I said, feeling my stomach flutter.

"What? That's good news. It means Adam's off the hook and everything's back to normal."

"I guess you're right," I said, still looking out at the buoy-studded water. A lobster boat chugged by slowly, and it looked like everything really was back to normal. But it still didn't feel resolved to me. For starters, I still didn't know who had left that horrid thing on my porch steps. And there were still all kinds of trouble down at the co-op.

"Did you ever hear anything from Eli, by the way?" Charlene asked.

"No," I said. "I've been meaning to check in with him, but with everything going on, I haven't gotten to it. Maybe I'll stop by on my way back from the Art Guild."

"The Art Guild? Why are you going over there?"

"I signed up for that awful pottery class with Catherine, so we're going for our second session. Speaking of Catherine, she wants to talk to you about online dating."

"Moving on already, eh?"

"Looks like it."

"Sarah and Murray were in here just this morning," she said. "It didn't look chummy."

"No?"

"He was trying to tell her she should use laminate flooring instead of real wood. He kept touching her arm, and she kept looking at him like he was a barnacle she was hoping to pry off as soon as possible."

"I can sympathize," I said. "So it didn't look romantic?"

"Not from her side, anyway. He was full of enthusiasm. I'm not sure if it's so much about her as the idea of a new development project; it's been a while since he's had anything to work on."

"Which is good news for the island," I said.

"True," Charlene agreed. "I'm kind of glad Catherine's moving on, frankly. She was a good influence on him, but I'm still not his biggest fan."

"Me neither," I said. "But I don't like to see her hurt."

"I hear you," she said. "We've both been there, haven't we? But we found love in the end."

"That's true," I said. "There's hope."

"Oh—and the Bermans were in, too. They're a piece of work, aren't they?"

"All three of them?" I asked.

"All three of them," she confirmed. "Chad Senior was upbraiding Chad Junior about keeping family matters in the family. Any idea what he was he talking about?"

"Nope," I said. "Did Chad say anything about Quartz?"

"No," she said. "But he looked kind of sick. Almost like he was in shock or something."

My antennae went up. "Really?"

"Yeah," she said. "I know you thought he wasn't really in to her, but maybe he liked her more than he let on."

Or maybe he had killed Chelsea after all, I thought privately.

"Love is weird, isn't it?" Charlene said.

"I can't argue with that," I said, still thinking about Chad. I was planning to ask him a few questions about Quartz at the Art Guild today. I wondered if his parents would still be hovering now that an arrest had been made. I decided odds were good.

"Anyway, let me know what you find out about Claudette," Charlene said, bringing me out of my reverie.

"I will," I said, pushing my chair back from the desk and standing up. "Keep your fingers crossed that Gwen's forgiven me."

"I'm sure everything will be fine. Are you going to ask about doing that co-op advertising?"

"We'll see how it goes," I said.

"All right. Keep me posted," she said, and signed off.

CHAD HADN'T ARRIVED at the Art Guild by the time we got there. I'd enjoyed the walk, but even though the Guild was a place of hope and promise for Gwen, it still made me a bit sad. I sniffed the roses blooming at the end of the driveway; they reminded me of Fernand, who had been Gwen's mentor and owned the place before meeting an untimely death.

"I'm going to pop in to see Gwen for a moment," I told Catherine, who had changed into tailored jeans and a taupe cotton blouse. Not exactly grubby clothes from my perspective, but probably easier to care for than cashmere.

"Sure. Tell her hi for me; I'll meet you in the pottery studio," Catherine said as we walked in the door.

"Will do."

I found Gwen in her small but bright studio, busy framing some of her recent work. Today, she wore jeans and one of Adam's oversize Cranberry Island T-shirts, her curly hair tied up in a knot on the top of her head. A sketch was taped to an easel by the window, and a mostly finished painting of a stand of lupines was taped to a board on her worktable; the focus on flowers made me wonder if she was taking inspiration from her fellow artist Emma. She looked up at me with a tentative smile when I walked in.

"These are beautiful," I said, pointing to the painting of lupines. The rich purple mixed with the pale green of the leaves and the gray-blue sky above was dreamy and lush. It had a different feel from her other work. "I've never seen you do a painting of just lupines before."

"I've been learning from Emma," she said. "I felt like experimenting; not to work to someone else's specifications, but to kind of express... I don't know. A feeling."

"Whatever it is, it's working," I said. She'd experimented before at the advice of another artist, trying to create what he considered more "commercial," with rather disastrous results. This, on the other hand, had a lovely, luminous feeling to it, and was anything but a disaster.

"I love having other artists around," she said as I admired the use of color in her new painting. "I'm so glad I was able to start the Guild; I think it's really helped me grow as an artist."

"You're always amazing," I said, "but I'm glad you're enjoying exploring a new direction, and your work is just beautiful."

"Thanks," she said, the corners of her mouth pulling up into a smile. "I'm sorry I was so hard on you on the phone. It was really upsetting, but I should have known you wouldn't do anything like that to Adam or me."

"I'm sorry I was so careless," I said. "I'm glad it's all worked out."

"Me too," she said. "I was terrified they were going to arrest Adam."

"You must have been," I replied. "By the way, I heard they found the *Carpe Diem*."

"Thank goodness, yes, they did," Gwen said, looking relieved. "Eli said he'll be back in the water by Monday. He's making Adam his top priority."

"Good," I said.

"And they arrested someone for that murder, so Adam's completely in the clear."

"I never doubted," I said.

She cocked a dark eyebrow. "Really?"

"Really," I reassured her. As I spoke, a thought occurred to me. "Hey... did Chelsea Sanchez ever talk to you about the Art Guild?"

"Funny you should ask," Gwen said. "She called about it last week, a few days before she got here. Said she had an interest in art, and wondered if she could stop by to check it out. I'd forgotten till you asked."

"Did she ask anything specific about it?"

"She asked who had founded it, and when," she said. "I told her I had started it, with funding from donors."

"Did she ask who the donors were?"

"She did, actually. I told her the name of the major donors—namely, the Bermans. I mentioned it to Chad, and he wasn't too happy about it."

"No?"

"In fact, he was really angry. Said his parents didn't want that information out, and I should have checked with them before saying anything." She sighed. "He's probably right. I don't know why he's so worried about it, though."

"I have an idea why. Apparently, Chelsea outed him in the school paper at Middlesex College," I informed Gwen. "His parents bought his admission to the college by buying a building."

"What?" Gwen put down the painting she was framing. "That's horrible! Did he know that's how he got in?"

"I don't know, but evidently it was a bit of a sore spot. Given Chelsea's background, I'm wondering if she was here undercover as a reporter, in fact."

"Have you looked her up?"

"I haven't gotten around to it, to be honest," I admitted. Which was kind of shortsighted of me.

"Let's do it now," Gwen said. "The computer's in the office."

I followed her into a small room loaded with papers, files, and art supplies. She opened her laptop and typed in Chelsea's name.

"I don't see anything here about Chelsea being a fisheries observer," she said. "In fact, the only Chelsea Sanchez I can find is a wrestler."

I looked over her shoulder at a picture. "That's not our Chelsea."

"No," she said. "It's not." She looked through Facebook, but none of the faces in the photos were familiar. "Let's check LinkedIn," she suggested.

There were no fisheries observers named Chelsea Sanchez on LinkedIn.

"Looks like she *was* here undercover," I said. "What's the name of the Middlesex College paper?"

She typed in a search. "The *Middlesex Campus*," she said.

"Google Chad Berman and *Middlesex Campus*," I suggested.

She typed in the names, and an article popped up... authored by a Chelsea Gutierrez. "Found it," Gwen said. Together, we scanned the article. It was as bad as Quartz had said it was, and must have been humiliating for Chad at the time. "Now let's do a search for Chelsea Gutierrez," I suggested.

She typed in the name. A profile for Chelsea Gutierrez, reporter for the *Portland Press Herald*, popped up.

At least that was one mystery solved, I thought. Unfortunately, it didn't get me any closer to figuring out who had killed her.

21

"*L*ooks like whoever pegged her as an undercover reporter was right," my niece said.

"But what was she working on?"

"Maybe she was doing a follow-up on Chad and the Art Guild?" Gwen suggested.

"That seems like awfully small potatoes for the Portland paper," I said. "I think it's got something to do with all the squabbling at the lobster co-op. After all, she was posing as a fisheries observer, not an artist."

"True," Gwen said.

"And if she was going undercover to out Chad, why wouldn't the paper send someone else? He obviously recognized her."

"Another good point," Gwen said, staring at the profile of Chelsea on the screen. "So what was she investigating?"

"She was supposed to be on Mac's boat," I said.

"And she died before she got on it," Gwen said. "Plus, all the boats being cut free..."

"Someone was trying to cover their tracks," I said.

Gwen looked at me, her face pale against her dark curls. "So did they arrest the wrong person?"

"I don't know," I said, "but I think it's a good possibility."

She let out a low, deep breath and stared at the picture on the screen. Chelsea had been so alive. And now..."What do we do?"

"I don't know," I said. "And the other thing that doesn't make sense is Quartz. She had nothing to do with the co-op. Why kill her?"

"Could there be two murderers?" Gwen suggested.

"The MO seems too similar."

"Unless whoever attacked Quartz imitated what happened to Chelsea to cover his or her tracks."

"I don't think the details of what happened to Chelsea were common knowledge," I said.

Gwen gave me a look. "Everything that happens on this island is common knowledge. I know how she died, and you didn't even tell me."

"True," I said. "But I still feel like we're missing something."

"So what do we do?"

"I've got pottery class in a minute," I said, glancing at the clock on the wall. "Let's talk about it afterward."

"Okay," she said. "How's class going, by the way?"

I gave her a look.

"I know," she said, wincing. "He's not great, is he?"

"Hard to say," I said diplomatically. "I guess I was more interested in making useful items than art objects. Then again, I'm not an artist," I said.

"I am an artist," she said in a low voice, "and I don't think he's very good, either. But sometimes you have to do what you have to do."

"I get it," I said. "Paying the bills is always a good thing." I stood up, still thinking about what we'd discovered about Chelsea. If I called the paper, would they tell me what story she was working on? Probably not, I decided; they'd decide to pursue it another way. What was she looking in to? Was there more going on with the local fishery than I realized? I thought again about the hidden compartment in the *Lucky Lady*. Were the lobstermen of Cranberry Island involved in illegal practices that would damage the fishery?

I thought again of the mortgage company notice I'd seen Tom Lockhart pick up at the store. I knew he was the head of the co-op; had he encouraged or enabled illegal practices to line his pockets? And was that why he was trying to keep the investigation from going beyond the island?

Even if he had, though, it still didn't explain what had happened to Quartz.

I was still thinking these thoughts as I headed into the studio where Catherine and Emmeline were already seated, chatting.

Five minutes before class was about to start, the sound of arguing came from the hallway.

"It's too much."

I recognized Chad's voice. A deeper male voice answered. "What do you mean, it's too much? It's what you wanted."

"I never wanted that," Chad answered.

"But sweetheart..." A woman's voice. "Everything your dad has done has been for you."

"Don't lay that on me," Chad said. "Nobody asked my opinion. Anyway, I've got to go. I have a class to teach."

"Only because of us," the deeper voice said. The condescension and menace in it made my skin crawl.

"Honey..." It was the woman's voice again. It was only one word, but the fear and supplication running through it made me shiver. The Bermans might look like they had it all, but at that moment, I was glad I was not Mrs. Berman.

"Don't 'honey' me," the deeper voice commanded.

"I didn't mean to upset you... it's just... there are people here..." she said in a cajoling tone. "Let's go outside to talk."

The man said, "I suppose you're right." Then, a moment later, "Son?" It sounded more like a command than a question.

There was no response. A moment later, a flustered Chad came through the door of the studio.

"Hey," he said in a distracted voice, then put on a bright smile, his eyes flitting only briefly to the door, as if he were expecting his father to storm through it. "Let's get out our projects from last time, okay? I'm going to give you a few minutes to get reacquainted with them."

I glanced through the window. Outside, Chad's parents were striding down the walkway, his father in the lead with his mother a few paces behind. Something about her posture put me in mind of a child who had been recently reprimanded. There was no question who ruled the Berman household—and fear and intimidation appeared to be the favored tactics.

As I retrieved my lump of clay, I watched Chad out of the corner of my eye. He was still flustered. I was guessing he didn't usually stand up to his father, and the experience must have upset him. What was he upset with his father about? Was there an argument over the funding of the Art Guild? Had Chad not known they were footing the bill? I knew Gwen knew it, but until the paper got wind of it, it hadn't been common knowledge.

All these thoughts percolated as we "worked," trying to form our clay wads into something artful. I really wanted to make a mug, but what I ended up with reminded me of an ashtray I'd made in second-grade art class. Catherine was having more luck with a vase, but I could sense she was still frustrated with the relative lack of instruction.

Chad looked agitated. About halfway through class, he excused himself for a few minutes and left the room. I looked at Catherine. "What do you think that was all about?" I asked in a low voice.

"I don't know," she said. "Maybe the funding?"

I thought about what Quartz had said. Maybe she'd told Chad his parents were funding the Art Guild? Maybe he'd thought she was saying he wasn't good enough, and hit her in a fit of anger? Had seeing Chelsea dredged up those old feelings again, too?

A shiver passed through me as I worked the cold clay. Was our art teacher—and Gwen's employee—actually a murderer after all?

I was still contemplating that awful thought when Chad returned. "I'm afraid I'm going to have to leave class early," he said. "Something's come up. You're welcome to work as long as you want... just be sure to wrap up your clay and put it on the shelf."

"But... we haven't learned anything!" Emmeline said.

He seemed about to answer, then thought better of it and walked out of the room, leaving Emmeline, Catherine, and me staring at one another.

"If Gwen weren't running the place, I'd ask for a refund," Catherine said.

"I'm going to go talk with her," I said. "Find out what's going on."

"Let us know, okay?" Emmeline said.

GWEN WAS FINISHING FRAMING her painting when I got to the studio.

"What's going on with Chad?" I asked.

"He quit," she said. "He said he was going to finish out the day and he was done."

"He just walked out of class," I informed her.

She muttered something under her breath, then said, "That was unprofessional of him."

"I know. Did he say why he was quitting?"

"Personal reasons," she said with a shrug. "It wasn't a very popular class anyway. I'll go talk to the students... I just hope it doesn't affect our funding."

"I noticed Chad's parents were here just before class."

She nodded. "They swung by to check in," she said. "See how the Guild was doing."

"I wonder what they're doing out here," I said. "I thought they were staying on Mount Desert Island."

"I think they rented a place out by the lighthouse," she told me. "The big blue house looking over the water."

"They didn't rent it for Chad?"

"Maybe they're staying with him," she said. "They seem a bit... overprotective. They remind me a little bit of my mom. Although at least they're supporting his art career."

"How much work has he done since he got here?" I asked.

"He's really not in the studio much," she admitted. "I almost feel as if he likes the idea of being an artist more than actually being an artist. Quartz sure seemed smitten with him."

"I KNOW. I hope she's doing okay, after what happened."

"She hasn't come to yet," I told her. "I'm hopeful, though."

"Poor thing," Gwen said. "I'd better go talk to the class. Thanks for letting me know. And please keep me posted if you find anything else out."

"Of course," I said.

"ARE you heading back to the inn?" Catherine asked after Gwen had finished talking to the class and we'd put our clay clumps back on the shelf. Gwen had told us she was going to try to find another instructor; if she couldn't, our money would be refunded.

Now, as we stepped out into the sunny afternoon, I said, "I think I'm going to go for a walk." I was actually thinking of paying Chad a visit, but I didn't want Catherine along; I had a feeling he'd be more open if it was just me.

"That sounds nice; I think I may head to the store to talk to Charlene about online dating. I'll take care of the rooms when I get back to the inn. Do you have dinner taken care of?"

"John's cooking tonight," I said.

"You have the night off, then," she said. "I think you need it!"

"I do," I agreed. "See you back at the inn? I may swing by a friend's house on the way back," I added, thinking of Eli and Claudette, "so I'll probably be an hour or two."

"I'll be there... along with Sarah," she told me, and a shadow passed over her face. She might be over Murray intellectually, but I knew there was still some more emotional work to do.

"Are you doing okay with everything?" I asked.

"Up and down," she said, averting her eyes. "I know it'll get better, but sometimes..."

"I understand," I said, reaching to touch her arm.

"Thanks," she said, looking up at me. "Thanks for being there. I know you know I thought you two were crazy for moving to this island, but you've been so kind to me, and so gracious, letting me in to your lives."

"We love you," I said. "You're family."

Her eyes teared up, and she pulled me into a hug. I was so startled—John's mom wasn't much of a hugger—that it took me a second to respond. I held her thin frame for a long time before she relaxed and moved away from me, dabbing at her eyes. "Thank you," she said in a husky voice.

"Anytime," I said. "I mean that."

"I know," she said, giving me a grateful smile.

I was still thinking about Catherine when I got to the big blue house by the lighthouse. It had a commanding view of the rocky beach below, and seemed awfully big for one person; it wasn't much smaller than the inn, from the look of it. Nor was it cheap. I wondered how Chad was feeding himself, then realized his parents had probably hired a personal chef, too. I almost felt sorry for him. Then I remembered the offhanded way he'd talked about Quartz and got over it.

I pushed the button beside the gray-painted door, and a sonorous doorbell sounded inside. I was about to ring the bell a second time when there was a shadow beside the stained-glass sidelights; a moment later, the door squeaked open, and Chad stood there.

"Can I help you?" he asked, looking confused.

"I wanted to ask you a few questions, if you don't mind."

"About what?"

"Can I come in for a minute?" I asked. "I'm dying for a glass of water."

"Ummm... sure," he said after a moment's hesitation. I

stepped into the cool interior, admiring the plank wood floors and the bank of windows along the back of the house. As I followed him to the kitchen, I said, "This is a really nice house."

"Thanks," he replied. "I'd really rather be at the inn, though. Your food's really good," he said with a sheepish smile. "I'd ask for a recipe for those apple pancakes, but I don't know how to cook." The good-looking, arrogant young man seemed abashed somehow... uncertain. He'd just cut some serious apron strings from his parents, I reasoned; no wonder he wasn't his normal confident self. Even though I still wasn't sure he didn't have something to do with what had happened to Chelsea and Quartz, I felt a bit of tenderness and compassion for him.

"I could teach you sometime if you like," I offered.

"To cook?"

"To make apple puff pancakes, anyway," I said as he grabbed a glass from one of the painted cabinets next to the enormous farm-style sink and filled it with ice and water. He handed it to me, and I took a grateful swig.

"So," he said. "I'm guessing you don't want to talk about cooking?"

"Not really," I said, shaking my head. "I'm curious about the barrette I found in your room, for starters."

"Oh, that barrette. You got me into a lot of trouble with that," he said, then caught himself.

"So you talked with Quartz the day she died," I said.

"Damn," he said. "I wasn't supposed to say anything."

"No? According to whom?" I asked as I slid onto one of the metal barstools at the mile-long soapstone island.

"Never mind," he said. "Anyway, the barrette belonged to Emma. I asked her about how she'd made it into some of the galleries she's in. She came over to my room for a few minutes. I guess she must have dropped it."

"Right by the bed?"

"I promise," he assured me. "I didn't sleep with Emma."

"But you weren't as crazy about Quartz as she was about you."

"Of course not," he said. "My parents would never let me..." He trailed off, catching himself. "She was fun, but not the kind of person I was interested in for a long-term relationship."

"She was interested in you, though," I said.

"Lots of women are," he said. "I come from a wealthy family, I've got a cool job..."

I took another sip of water. "Not anymore," I reminded him.

"True," he said.

"What are you going to do to support yourself?" I asked, knowing full well he didn't have to.

"I don't know yet," he said, looking very young and very lost. Gone was the callow youth on the phone with a friend, dissing Quartz; now he looked like a troubled young man. Had the two deaths caused a true sea change in him?

Or was he just a very, very good actor?

22

"*I* heard you arguing with your parents earlier," I said.

"Oh," he said, flushing.

"Sounds like things have been tough lately."

"They just... they just *do* things without consulting me," he said. "Always for my own good."

"Like the issue at Middlesex College?"

His face turned an even darker pink. "You know about that?"

"Chelsea wrote the article, didn't she?"

"She did," he said. "Just because she couldn't afford to study art. She was angry that she didn't have the same options I did. As far as she was concerned, I was pretty privileged."

From what I could see, he *was* pretty privileged.

"What made her choose you?" I asked. "I'm sure you weren't the only one."

"We had a one-night stand after a gallery field trip," he said. "I didn't call." He shrugged. "I guess it made her mad."

"I guess so," I said. "Any idea why she was here on the island?"

"My parents thought she was writing another article about me and the Art Guild." He snorted. "Ridiculous. If that guy at the inn hadn't offed her, they would have figured out it was crazy." The old Chad was back for a moment. "Why did he off her, anyway? I assumed it was one of the locals, with all the boats cut loose and everything. I hear someone thought she was some kind of policeman."

"I'm not privy to all the facts," I said.

"Maybe he was bonking both of them," he said. "Chelsea and Quartz. Maybe his girlfriend found out."

I tried to hide my distaste and returned to an earlier subject. "Quartz wasn't too happy about that barrette, was she?"

"Nope. She came to the Art Guild practically in hysterics. We were supposed to go for a walk, but she was so mad, we didn't even get out of my studio."

"So you argued at the Guild?"

"Yeah," he told me. "I didn't realize she was taking things so seriously. It was just fun. It wasn't like we were planning to get married or anything."

"She thought you were, I think."

He glanced up at me, then looked to the side.

"Did she know about the Art Guild and the fact that your parents funded it?"

"Yeah," he said. "She heard Gwen talking about it. She kind of threw it in my face."

"What do you mean?"

"She called me... some not nice things," he told me. "She was upset. I'm sure she didn't mean them."

"How did you part ways?"

He shrugged. "I told her it was over and she stormed out of the place."

"You didn't follow her?" I asked. I wanted to ask about the money in her hand, but I wasn't sure how to do it without revealing information I shouldn't.

He shook his head. "No," he said. "My dad was..."

"What?"

"Nothing," he said.

"He wasn't a fan of Quartz, was he?"

Chad averted his eyes. "He didn't really take it seriously."

"It's been tough, being his son, hasn't it?"

"It has," he said, and looked up at me, suddenly guarded. "Why am I talking to you, anyway? I hardly know you."

"It's been a rough week," I suggested. "Sometimes it's good to talk."

"I guess," he said. "But I probably shouldn't."

"Why not?"

"I don't like to talk about family matters," he said.

He seemed defensive, but I'd just asked if his dad liked Quartz. I was beginning to have some serious doubts about Chad's father. I thought again about the wad of money in Quartz's hands... and her comment about "not good enough." A disturbing thought occurred to me. Had Chad's father killed Chelsea because he thought she was going to write another exposé on his son? And had he tried to murder Quartz because he thought she wasn't good enough for him? Or that, in her anger, she was going to expose his son's incompetence somehow?

"I should probably get to work on a few things," Chad said, taking my water glass from me.

"Got it," I said. "I'll head out, then." As I stood up, there was a knock on the door. Chad looked sick, but didn't move to answer it.

He didn't need to, as it turned out. I heard the sound of a key in the lock, and a moment later, his mother's voice sounded. "Sweetheart? Are you here?"

"I'm here, Mom."

"Good. I was hoping you'd reconsider," she said, her voice coming closer. "Those women were just trying to hold you back. That's why your father tried with the money first..."

Chad's face turned to a look of horror as she rounded the doorway to the kitchen.

"Oh," she said, blinking. "I didn't know you had company."

"She's just leaving," he said.

"I am," I said. "But what did you mean about those women?"

"Just..."

As she spoke, there was another knock on the door, and it opened.

"Chad," his father bellowed.

Mrs. Berman turned pale. "Oh, goodness," she murmured, and her hand leaped to her mouth.

It was time for me to leave, I decided.

"Well, I've got to run," I announced. "Thanks for the water."

"But you can't go," his mother said, her eyes wide; for all her expensive clothing and makeup, she reminded me of a startled rabbit.

"Why not?" Chad asked, looking agitated. "Look, Mom..."

"Why is she here?" Chad's father asked as he strode into the kitchen.

"Your son gave me a glass of water," I said, feeling adrenaline pulse through me. What had I gotten myself in to? "I'm just on my way out. Good to see you," I said.

"Oh, Charles," Chad's mother said. I had no idea what her name was, I realized. "I think I made a mistake."

"Again?" he asked. "What is it this time, Julia?"

"She heard me," she said in almost a whisper, wincing as she spoke.

"Heard you say what?" he asked in a menacing tone that made my skin crawl. Disguised under the light Polo shirt, neatly pressed khakis, and Docksiders, I saw now, was a man who seethed with anger.

"It's nothing, Dad," Chad said, stepping toward his mother. "Everything's fine."

But Chad's father's eyes never swayed from his wife's. "Heard you say what?" he repeated in a tone that made my mouth dry up and my heart rate double. Chad's mother cringed, putting up her hands over her head, and I suddenly wondered if her foundation might be disguising something other than aging skin.

"I'm so sorry," she whispered. "She heard... she heard me say something about those women... and money."

"Jesus. You are such a moron," he said. "Man. Now I know where this one here gets it from." He shot a contemptuous glance at his son, whose face burned, as he towered over his wife. He raised his hand as if to hit her, then spotted me and smoothed down his hair instead. "All I do is try to save you from mistakes," he said, turning to Chad. "I give you opportunities you never could have earned for yourself, and then you squander them and shame me. You must take after your mother," he said, sending a contemptuous glance at Julia, who flinched.

"Dad..."

Charles ignored him. "I try to help you establish yourself. Try to keep you from getting mixed up with some gold-digging dingbat. Save you from making the mistakes I made.

And what do you do?" He clenched his fist. "You spit in my face."

This was a family conversation I had no desire to be privy to. I glanced around, looking for a way out, but Charles was standing between me and the only exit I knew of. Julia looked absolutely terrified. So did Chad, but there was a streak of defiance I admired. I'd felt almost disdainful of Chad and his apparently easy life, but I now saw him with fresh eyes. Chad's life wasn't exactly the bed of roses I'd imagined. Or if it was, it came with some rather nasty thorns.

Not just nasty, I thought as I looked at Charles Berman, whose face was contorted with anger to the point where he was almost unrecognizable.

I started to edge away from the soapstone island in the direction of the front door, hoping Charles was so focused on his family that he wouldn't notice.

Unfortunately, that wasn't how it worked out.

"Where do you think you're going?" he spat at me.

"I just thought I'd let myself out," I said quietly.

"Sit down," he ordered, pointing to the barstool I'd vacated. I decided that would be the best course of action, at least for now, and found myself wishing I'd told Catherine I was coming to visit Chad.

"Now," Charles said, addressing his wife and son again, in a silky-smooth, condescending tone that could have curdled milk. "You've gotten us into trouble yet again. How do you propose we get ourselves out of it?"

"I don't know what you mean," Chad said.

"She knows about the money I gave that slutty girlfriend of yours to keep her mouth shut and go away," Charles said in a harsh tone. "And unless she's a total idiot, she's probably putting a few other things together in her head right now."

"Really," I said, starting to get up again. "I don't have any idea what you're talking about. I shouldn't be here."

"Sit," he barked again.

I sat, but as he turned back to face his wife and son, I reached in my pocket for my phone. I had slid it out of my pocket and had started texting John when a fist came down on the counter next to me. I jumped, and the phone skittered out of my hand and across the floor.

Chad's father snatched it off the floor and read my text out loud. "'At blue house by the lighthouse. In trouble, Chad's....'"

"Give me back my phone, please," I said.

"Give you back your phone?" He let out a derisive snort. "You don't know what trouble is. Who else knows you're here?"

"Catherine," I lied. "My mother-in-law."

"If she knows, then why are you telling this John guy—" he glanced down at my phone again "—he's the deputy. Your husband, right? Anyway, why are you having to tell him where you are?"

The words tumbled out of my mouth too fast. "I don't know if he's talked with Catherine yet."

"And you think they're going to come to save you." He put my phone in the back pocket of his khakis, and my stomach sank. "We're done here," he said in a cold voice.

"That's fine," I said, trying not to sound as if my blood was running cold. "If you just give me back my phone, I'll go."

"Give you back your phone," he said. "So you can go run off to your husband and tell him to reopen the investigation? I don't think so."

"They've already arrested someone," I reminded him.

He shook his head. "Doesn't matter. You're a liability now."

"Charles," Julia said in a wobbly voice, looking pale. "I don't think this is a good idea."

"Shut up," he said in a flat voice, without turning around.

"Dad," Chad said. "She's right. This has gone too far."

Charles turned to his son, his jaw set, his face dangerously red. "This is all your doing. Everything that's happened is because of you. It's all been for you. Are you really willing to throw everything away after all I've done for you?"

"Dad... I never asked for..."

"No," Charles spat. "Of course not. You just expected it. And now that it's getting uncomfortable, you're going to wuss out. I should have known."

"I didn't want any of this!" Chad protested.

"Ingrate!" Charles spat. "I sacrificed for you. I gave you all the opportunities I never had. And you've done nothing but throw it back in my face."

"I never asked you to kill anyone."

I swallowed hard. If I wasn't in the soup before, I was now.

Charles didn't deny it. To the contrary, in fact. "If you'd been able to keep yourself from being shamed, I wouldn't have had to!" he bellowed. "Your reputation would be mud without me. How much do you think your pieces would have gone for after that girl wrote another exposé about you? I already get enough crap from my golfing buddies because you're an artist." His upper lip curled in contempt. "A failed artist? I could never show my face again."

Chad's face turned red with shame.

"No," Charles said. "I couldn't let that happen. And then, shacking up with that girl... and marrying her!"

"I wasn't going to marry her," Chad said.

"That's not what she said," Charles told him. "She was plotting to get pregnant and trap you. I know the type," he added, glancing over at Julia. "How do you think you ended up here?"

"Charles!" Julia said, looking horrified.

"It's the truth, Julia," Charles said. "It's your fault he's a total failure."

"He's not," Julia said. "He's very talented. His third-grade art teacher..."

"Third-grade art teacher? Really? I think we're done here," he said, and turned to Chad. "But this is the last time I go to bat for you. Next time, you're on your own."

"I don't want you to go to bat for me," Chad said. "I never wanted you to. Not like this."

"You sure didn't complain when I got you into that fancy school."

"I didn't know!" Chad said. "It was so embarrassing... I wanted to crawl into a hole when I saw that article. I had no idea you'd pulled strings to get me accepted."

"You never even thanked me."

Chad crossed his arms over his chest, a mix of fury and fear on his face. "I'd rather not get in at all than have you buy me a spot without telling me. It wasn't fair."

"Fair?" Spittle spewed from Charles's mouth as he spoke. "I bend over backward for you, and it isn't fair?"

Julia put a tentative hand on her husband's arm. "Charles..."

He whirled to face his wife, slapping her hand away. "I said, shut up!"

She took a step backward, her face sheet white, cradling her hand against her chest.

"I think we need a breather," Chad suggested.

"No," Charles said. "We need to deal with the situation." He turned to me. "You. We're going for a walk."

"If you kill me like you did the others, they'll know they have the wrong murderer," I pointed out as calmly as I could, trying to buy time.

"Like I hadn't thought of that. You're a regular genius, aren't you?" he said. "No loss to the gene pool with you gone."

"Leave her out of this," Chad said, stepping toward him.

"It's too late for that," Charles said. "Surely even you can see that." He turned back to me. "Now, let's go."

"Where are we going?" I asked.

"For a walk," he said shortly. "Come on."

"Charles..."

"I'll be back in fifteen minutes," he said, glancing at his watch.

"I'm not going," I said. After all, he didn't have a gun. I stood up and made a break for the door, but he caught my arm. I tried to wrench myself free, but his hand was like a vise just above my elbow.

"Let me go," I said, yanking on my arm.

"No," he said, yanking me over toward the countertop.

"Dad! Stop it," Chad commanded. Julia just stood there, wide-eyed, apparently paralyzed.

Charles ignored his son and yanked open a drawer, rifling through the contents until he pulled out a shiny meat mallet.

"You wouldn't," Julia breathed as he raised the mallet in one swift motion, then brought it down toward my head. I flinched and lunged to the side, but it still smacked me above my left ear. The kitchen wobbled, and my knees buckled beneath me.

I jerked my head, up, expecting to see Charles raising the mallet for a second blow, but as I hit the floor, I heard the word "No!"

Chad launched himself across the kitchen, smashing into his father. The mallet tumbled from his grip, hitting the wood floor with a bang; at the same time, the grip on my arm loosened. I pulled free and scrambled away from the two men, who were now writhing on the floor with Julia standing nearby, staring at them.

"Charles! No!" she screamed as Charles's hand reached out toward the mallet.

I tried to get to my feet, but I was too dizzy. As Chad struggled to keep his father down, the older man's hand crept closer and closer to the mallet. I was horrified. Would he really kill his son?

As I watched, Charles rolled toward the mallet, taking his son with him. His fingers closed on the handle, and he pulled it up, raising it over his son's head.

Before he could swing it, there was a crash. A potted fern exploded on Charles's head. The man went limp, the mallet tumbling to the hardwood floor.

Above him stood his wife, Julia.

23

"Oh, no," she whispered, her whole body shaking. "Is he... did I hurt him?"

She'd just dropped a potted plant on the man's head, so odds were the answer was yes, but I wasn't about to scold her.

Chad disentangled himself from his father, looking like he was still in shock, then stood up and wrapped an arm around his mother.

"I didn't mean to hurt him," she said in a small voice. "I just... he was going to hurt my boy. And I couldn't let him do it."

"I know, Mom," he said. "I know."

As they spoke, I crawled over to Charles and touched his neck. He had a pulse, thank goodness. On the downside, that meant he could come to at any minute.

I fished my phone out of his pocket and called John. He answered on the second ring.

"John, I'm at the blue house by the lighthouse. I need you to get the van and come now."

"Why? What happened?"

"Charles Berman just..." I looked up at the stricken faces of his wife and son. "Well, I'll explain when you get here. Just come. Quickly."

"Are you okay?" he asked.

"I am. For now," I said, and hung up. "Do you have any rope, or twine, or anything?"

Julia blinked. "Why?"

"In case he comes to, I'd like to make sure he can't do something like that again."

"You're going to tie him up?" Julia asked, then seemed to reconsider. "Yes. It seems cruel, but you're right." She gave her son a hug. "I can't risk my boy."

"I saw some rope in the garage, I think, hanging by the door," Chad said.

"Where's the garage?"

"Down that hallway and to the right," he said, pointing beyond the Sub-Zero fridge, and looked at me. "I'll keep an eye on Mom and Dad, if you'll run and get it."

"Are you sure you're okay?" I asked.

He nodded. "I'll be fine," he said. "Go."

I hurried down the hallway and opened the door to the garage; thankfully, it was right where Chad remembered it being. I grabbed the coil of white-cotton rope from a nail on the wall and ran back down the hallway to the kitchen, where Chad had rolled his father over.

I quickly trussed up his hands and feet, using the knots I'd learned to tie since moving to a seafaring community. Chad watched me, grim-faced and pale, and Julia cried into her hands.

As soon as Charles was secured to my satisfaction, I checked his pulse and breathing and brushed away soil and pottery shards to examine the wound on his head. He'd gotten quite a bump, but already his eyes were moving behind their lids, and he was groaning.

"Do you have an ice pack?" I asked.

"I don't know," Chad said.

"I can make one," Julia said, seeming almost happy to have a task to do. I watched as she dug a plastic bag out of the pantry and filled it with ice, then wrapped it in a dish towel and put it on his head. When she was done, she looked at a loss again, and stood with her arms wrapped around herself, rocking slightly. A moment later, she buried her head in her hands again, while Chad looked at me helplessly.

I stood up and went over to Julia, putting a hand on her shoulder. She flinched and jerked away, and my heart ached for her. Hers had clearly not been a happy or healthy marriage, and I suspected the effects would be long-lasting.

"You saved your son," I reminded her. She didn't remove her hands from her face.

"I almost killed Charles," she moaned.

"You didn't," I said. "You knocked him out while he was attacking Chad. You did what you had to do. He was going to hit your son over the head with a meat mallet."

"He gets angry, but he's never..." She swallowed hard. "Never that I saw, anyway. I mean, a little bit of shoving, and maybe things got a bit out of hand sometimes... but he never... never..."

"Killed anyone?" Chad said in a stricken voice. "But he did, Mom. Somebody died because of me."

"Not because of you," I corrected him.

"No? If I'd been a decent son, he wouldn't have had to do all those things for me."

"Everything he did was his choice," I told Chad. "You

didn't ask him to do any of the things he did. You didn't even know he did them."

"But..."

"No 'but.' He made the choices he made. He may have thought he made them to help you, but they were bad decisions, they were his decisions, and they were one-hundred percent his responsibility." Chad finally met my eyes, and I put my hands on his shoulders. "I promise, Chad. None of this is your fault."

"She's right," Julia said. "If anything, it's my fault. I didn't stop him. Didn't speak up."

"Did you know he was buying my way into Middlesex?"

She hesitated, then nodded. "I was scared to tell him no," she said in almost a whisper. "And then, with those girls... I didn't know until it was too late. And now I just... I feel like I should have said something earlier. That if I had..."

"You didn't know," I said.

"Of course she didn't know," Charles said from the floor. The ice pack slid to the side as he moved his head. "Why would I tell her? She'd be too stupid to keep her mouth shut."

Julia stared at him. "I can't believe I stayed with you so long. You're... you're a monster." She reached for Chad's arm. "I'm so sorry, sweetheart."

I was sorry, too. For both of them.

~

BY THE TIME the paramedics and the police took Charles away, Chad and Julia had both talked with the detective, and were sitting in the kitchen of their rental looking shell-shocked.

"Why don't you come back to the inn with us?" I offered, holding John's hand. "It'll be good to be around people."

"But they'll all know what happened."

I shrugged. "It wasn't your doing. Just come," I offered again. "You can have dinner in the kitchen with us if you'd like to avoid everyone else. I've got plenty of room and plenty of food."

They exchanged glances. "I... I think I'd like that, actually," Julia said. "I don't want to be anywhere that reminds me of him. Chad, will you come? I don't want to be alone."

"I'll come," he said. "Let me just get my stuff. I don't want to stay in the same room, though," Chad said. "It'll remind me... remind me of Quartz."

"We'll put you on a different floor," John promised.

After a long moment, Chad said, "Okay," and disappeared upstairs a minute later.

"Do you need to get anything?" I asked Julia. "You're welcome to borrow. Between Catherine and me, I'm sure we can cover you."

"Thank you," she said. "I don't have anything. It's all on the boat or the mainland. I'll come." A few minutes later, Chad and Julia climbed into the back of the inn's van, looking like survivors of a terrorist attack.

In a way, I reflected, they kind of were.

24

"So all's well that ends well," Charlene said as we walked over to watercolor class the next morning. Breakfast had been easy but delicious; I'd served my favorite overnight French toast recipe along with a fruit salad and eggs to order, and there had been lots of oohing and ahhing over the food, along with speculation over recent events. Chad and Julia had come down to breakfast a little late, but both had been embraced by the artists from the Guild, and had looked relieved and grateful for their compassion. Emma even offered to work with Chad a bit to help him market his work.

Now, as we walked along the road on a perfect Maine morning, I turned to Charlene and pointed out her error. "Not completely," I said. "I still feel horrible for Chelsea, and although Quartz came to briefly, she's still got a ways to go." I'd called the hospital that morning; Quartz's mother, who had arrived the day before, had given me an update.

"She'll recover, though, right?"

"She will," I confirmed. "But she, Chad, and Julia have a lot of healing to do."

"That's true," Charlene agreed. "It was all pretty horrible. Talk about a snowplow parent."

"I know," I said. "Charles confessed he used a motorboat to cut loose all the boats in the harbor, just to spread suspicion."

"What did he do, anyway?"

Charles had told us the details while we waited for the police. "After he saw Chelsea that night, he convinced himself she was planning to shame Chad again. He looked her up and confirmed that she was a reporter, then took a boat out during the night to cut loose the rest of the lobster boats—he had heard she was here on the island purportedly to go out on a lobster boat, and you know it's been in the news a bit."

"True," I said.

"So once he did that, he pulled his boat ashore and waited outside the inn for her to come out. She took the cliff path, and he followed her and killed her. He followed the same pattern with Quartz a few days later."

"Scary," she said.

"But that still doesn't explain who left that stuffed animal on my doorstep," I reflected. "And I have no idea what the deal was between Mac and Earl."

"I know what the deal was between Mac and Earl," Charlene said smugly.

"What?"

"Earl told Mac he had a problem and needed to go to rehab. Mac had had too much to drink, so he blew a gasket and plowed into his boat."

"Really?"

"Really," she said. "He just said the thing about blaming Earl for the observer because he didn't want to admit what had really happened. Apparently, he *was* fishing illegally to make enough money to support his habit, and I think a few locals knew he was doing it, so it was a reasonable explanation."

"Alcohol problem?"

"That and opioids," she said.

"Oof," I said. "That stuff is nasty."

"I know," she told me. "Another reporter from the Portland paper stopped by the shop to ask me some questions about what all had gone on; you'll probably hear from her, too. Turns out opioids are what Chelsea was here to report on."

"Not Chad and the Art Guild?" I shook my head. Chelsea had died to keep her from reporting on a story she wasn't even interested in.

"Nope. She was doing a big feature on opioid addiction in the lobster industry. There are a few here who are addicted... that's part of the reason there's been some cheating lately when it comes to fishing." She dabbed at her paper again and continued in a low voice. "Keep it under your hat, but Mac and Earl were doing a little illegal lobstering."

"That explains the hidden tank on Earl's boat," I said. "Why?"

"A little extra money, of course. A few extra traps set. But others got wind of it, and things started to get hot." She leaned in close and whispered to me, "Apparently, Mac was desperate enough for money that he just started selling a few illegal lobsters to a lobster pound over on Mount Desert Island."

"What are they going to do about it?"

"It can't be proved now—I think the evidence is eaten—but Tom has decided to deal with it on the island and not call the Marine Patrol."

"Are you sure Tom's not in on it?" I asked. "He had what

looked like a nastygram from a mortgage company the other day, remember?"

She blinked at me. "Wait. Are you suggesting Tom might be fishing illegally?" She laughed. "No. He's been trying to refinance for three months, but the old company hasn't gotten the memo and keep sending bills. He's at his wit's end."

"So he's not fishing illegally?"

"Of course not!" Charlene said.

"I'm relieved to hear that," I said, feeling a cloud lift. "Are people still talking about Adam?"

"No," she said. "I think he just had a good streak."

"Is Mac going to rehab?"

"They're checking him in today," Charlene told me. "I think ramming the *Lucky Lady* made him realize how bad things had gotten. His sister and Earl are taking him in."

"Does he know?"

"I don't know," Charlene said, "so I'm not going to broadcast it."

"Got it," I said.

"And speaking of which..." As we walked, three people came into view. Mac, trailing a rolling suitcase, Earl, and a woman I didn't recognize but must have been his sister.

"Hey," Charlene said.

Mac looked like he'd been rode hard and put up wet, as they used to say in Texas. So did Mac's sister; apparently, it hadn't been an easy process. Earl looked grim.

"Hey," I said.

Mac looked up at me, all the vitriol from the other day evaporated. "Sorry about what I left on your porch," he said. "And for that call."

"That was you?" I asked.

"I didn't want you messing around," he said. "I wouldn't have done anything bad. I just wanted to get you to shut up."

"Nice," Earl said.

"I was a desperate man," Mac said. "Anyway, I saw you over at Eli's. You always ask too many questions, and I wanted my private business quiet." He grimaced and glanced at his sister. "Although that hasn't worked out too well, thanks to you two."

"We love you," she said.

"Funny way of showing it, dragging me out of my house like this."

"Oh, don't be a wuss," Earl said. "You know you need help. And I'll check your traps while you're gone."

"Fine," he said in a gruff tone. "But I am not talking to any stinking reporters." Mac harrumphed and kept walking, and his sister hurried to catch up to him, as if she were afraid he'd change his mind and take a wrong turn.

"You're a good friend," I told Earl. "And she's a good sister."

"Tell him that," Earl said, nodding his head toward Mac, then stumped after Mac and his sister.

We stood watching them head down to the mail boat for a moment. "Well," Charlene finally said. "I think that resolves just about everything."

"Everything except the Art Guild. And Claudette," I said, with a sense of foreboding.

"We'll talk to Gwen about the situation with the Guild and drop by Claudette and Eli's after class," Charlene said. "We didn't do a very good job organizing meals this week, did we?"

"No, we didn't," I said.

"We have a perfect excuse to stop by, then," she pointed out.

WE GOT to the Art Guild a few minutes later, and Charlene and I detoured to Gwen's studio. My niece was putting the final touches on a painting of the lighthouse. She looked remarkably upbeat, considering her main donor had been arrested for murder.

"How's it going?" I asked.

"Oh, crazy as usual," she said, adding a touch of blue paint to intensify a shadow.

"I'm sorry about the loss of your donor," Charlene said.

"It's okay," she told us. "Chad called last night and told me what happened; it's tragic, but we'll be okay. His mom is going to pick up the slack; she might even take some art classes. She always wanted to, but her husband told her she wasn't very good." She grimaced. "It might be good therapy for her."

"I hope so," I said.

"In the meantime," she said, "I'm thinking I need to work on other types of funding, so if you've got time this week, Aunt Nat, I'd like to see if we can put together some art packages for later this summer or in the fall."

"Really?"

"Really," she said. "And I'll help with some of your marketing, too; I've learned a lot from one of those online artists' groups."

"Thank you," I said, resisting the urge to kiss Gwen right then and there.

"Now. We've got class in five minutes. Did you do the homework I assigned?"

"Uhh..." Charlene and I looked at each other.

"I guess I can give you a pass, considering the week you've had. But next time..."

"We'll do it," Charlene and I promised.

"Good," she said. "Now, let's go do some art!"

By the time we left the Art Guild, I was still terrible at painting, but I was feeling better than I had in days. Except for my worry about Claudette.

Eli wasn't in his workshop when we got to the Whites' house, which was surprising, considering the number of repairs I knew he had to make. Muffin and Pudge were in a fenced enclosure in the backyard; Pudge was testing the gate, and Muffin was nosing the fence.

Charlene knocked, and we glanced at each other as we waited. A moment later, Eli answered the door, looking cheerier than I'd seen him in weeks.

"It's two of my favorite ladies!" he said. "Outside Claudie, that is. Come in, come in!"

We followed him into the little house, which smelled of tea and books, and into the living room, where Claudette was tucked into a recliner with her knitting beside her.

"We just stopped by for a visit," Charlene said.

"And to find out about the tests, I imagine," Claudette said.

"Well?" Charlene asked impatiently. "Did you hear back?"

"She's clear," Eli said, his face splitting into a sunny smile.

"Oh, thank goodness," I said, feeling tension I didn't even know I was carrying leaving my body.

"The biopsy results came back negative," Claudette announced.

"But she's way low on iron," Eli said. "They thought it might be lymphoma, but anemia's why she's been so tired all the time, and the swollen nodes must have been from a virus. She was cutting back on red meat so much, she tanked her iron count."

"They have you on something to fix that?" I asked.

"They do," she said. "It'll take a bit, but my energy should come back. Between the low iron and the virus... the combination just knocked me out."

"I'm so glad it's not something worse," I said. "I think this calls for a celebration."

"Cookies?" Eli said hopefully, casting a glance at his wife.

"I think we can make an exception," Claudette said. "But we don't have any in the house."

"Actually..." Eli turned a bit pink, but said, "I'll be right back."

He disappeared into the kitchen and returned a moment later with a Baggie. "I tucked a few of your lemon bars into the freezer not too long ago. Hid 'em behind the green beans."

Claudette gave him a stern look—but not too stern. "Eli!"

"Just for an occasion such as this," he said, opening the bag and distributing frozen lemon bars. Even Claudette took one. He held up his lemon bar, dropping a bit of powdered sugar onto the rug. "To Claudette's health!" he announced.

"Hear, hear!" I said, and we all touched lemon bars, then dug in.

Even Claudette.

"CLAUDETTE'S CLEAR!" I announced when I walked into the inn kitchen twenty minutes later. Catherine and John were sitting at the table drinking tea.

"She is?" John asked, getting up and folding me into a hug. "That's great news!"

"I know. She's just really anemic and getting over a virus; they thought it might be lymphoma, but she's clear."

"Thank goodness," Catherine said.

"I also found out what's going on with Mac and Earl," I told him, and relayed the morning's encounter. "I don't know if it's public knowledge, though, so please don't say anything."

"Oh, it'll be public knowledge whether he wants it to be or not," John said. "But maybe we can all pitch in and help out."

"I hope so," I said, and turned to Catherine, who was looking springy in a pale pink blouse and white capris. "How are you?" I asked. I hadn't really talked to her since after class the day before.

"Doing surprisingly well," she said. "But what about you? You've had an exciting twenty-four hours."

"I have," I said, "but things are sorted now. I feel bad for Chad and Julia, though."

"It sounds like it was a horrific situation." Catherine took a sip of tea. "At least they can heal now. Although after living with that for so many years... it'll take time."

"I'm sure it will," I said. "How are you doing, by the way?"

"Well, I got my profile up, with Charlene's help," she said, then made a face. "Of course, Murray called right after I did it, and said he wants to have dinner."

"Are you going to go?" I asked.

"I'm not sure." She turned her cup around on the table as she spoke. "I think I need some time, too. Besides," she added, glancing up with a mischievous look in her eyes, "it might be fun to see what's out there."

"Whatever you decide, we're totally behind you," I said. "I just want you to be happy."

"Speaking of happy," John said, "you got a message back from that magazine you sent the scone recipe to."

"Uh-oh. What is it?"

"They'd like to come spend a weekend here, and maybe do a feature on the inn," he said.

"What? When?"

"Next weekend," he said.

"That would give us enough time to set something up with Gwen," I said. "Perfect for publicity."

"Maybe things are looking up after all," Catherine said.

"Maybe they are," I said with a smile, feeling a rush of gratitude for John, for Catherine, for the beauty of the island and the inn, for the warm community around me... and for the life I'd built for myself.

It wasn't always easy, but I wouldn't have it any other way.

SPELL OF TROUBLE

CHAPTER ONE

*"Y*ou have arrived at your destination."

"What?"

As if responding to the navigation system, Georgina, my stuffed-to-the-gills-and-a-little-bit-beyond, lima-bean-green Kia Soul, gave a soft sigh and shut down.

"No. No, no, no. My destination is Portland. PORTLAND. Not the side of a highway in the middle of nowhere."

It was raining. It was pitch black. I was the only person stupid enough to be on the road at 2 a.m. on a Tuesday night. And I was absolutely, positively, nowhere near my destination.

I took a deep breath as the car rolled onto the narrow shoulder, then put the car into park and turned the key in the ignition. Just as I turned it, a huge bolt of lightning forked down from the sky, illuminating the small exit sign a hundred yards in front of me.

EXIT 43A. MISTY HOLLOW.

I turned the key in the ignition again — nothing — and reached for my cell phone.

Which was also dead.

"Well, this is exciting," said Aunt Matilda from the seat next to mine.

"Easy for you to say," I told her. Since she was a ghost, she wasn't bothered by rain, the absence of chocolate bars, or the prospect of spending a long, wet night trying to sleep in the front seat of my car. "Any suggestions?"

"I'm just along for the ride," she replied. Aunt Matilda had been with me for the last two years. Neither of us was sure why she latched onto me after choking on an olive at the Svelte Seniors Picnic in Fort Myers, Florida a few years ago, but we'd come to something of a companionable arrangement.

"Brilliant," I said.

"Oh, cheer up. Maybe something good will come of it."

"Like a serial killer finding me stranded on the side of the road?"

"At least you wouldn't have to worry about paying for a hotel room," Aunt Matilda pointed out.

"That's certainly glass half-full," I said, looking at the rain-streaked windshield, which was faintly illuminated by a billboard advertising "Misty Hollow: Your destination for a magical vacation." The small billboard featured a picture of a fanciful witch on a broomstick and an overfed black cat in a red bow tie. The chamber of commerce could use some help, I thought. Maybe I should drop off a resume.

"You're worried about the job situation again, aren't you?" Aunt Matilda asked.

"When am I not worried about the job situation?"

"What happened to the taffy machine wasn't your fault," she said.

"Don't remind me," I groaned.

"And when you sent out the ad with the picture of the donkey on it... It could have happened to anyone. And who knew the gorilla was going to get free at the zoo just as you put on the banana suit?"

I knew she was trying to make me feel better, but going through a grand tour of my previous job mishaps wasn't doing much for my morale. "Are those headlights?" I asked, trying to interrupt her recitation of my checkered career.

They were. They came, and they went, leaving me alone with Aunt Matilda and all of my worldly possessions.

"At least it wasn't a serial killer," Aunt Matilda said cheerily.

I sighed. Now what? I was hours away from everyone I knew (well, everyone except Aunt Matilda), and hours away from where I wanted to be. My phone was dead. And I was stuck on a dark road in the middle of nowhere, at two in the morning, during a rainstorm.

I had just hit the hazard lights on my car when another pair of headlights appeared behind me on the road. As I watched, they pulled in behind me, illuminating the small slit at the top of the rearview mirror—the only part not obscured by my worldly possessions. I sat frozen in the car, watching in the side mirror as someone opened the door of the car behind mine, walked up beside me, and knocked on the window. I wasn't sure if I should be relieved or terrified.

"He doesn't look like a serial killer," Aunt Matilda observed.

"How can you tell?" I asked as he tapped on the window. He was wearing a raincoat that made it impossible to tell anything about him—I was guessing it was a him, since he seemed to be over six feet tall—and I was in a bit of a dilemma. I couldn't open the window—the car was dead— and the way my luck was going, I wasn't about to open the door. "Need help?" he shouted through the glass.

"I'm fine," I yelled back.

"Hogwash," Aunt Matilda retorted.

"I wasn't talking to you," I muttered.

The man paused and dug something out of his pocket. I prayed it wasn't a gun.

It wasn't. It was a badge.

"I promise I'm not an ax murderer," he said, as if he'd read my mind. I opened the door a bit so we could talk, and a sheet of cold water poured onto my leg. "What's wrong with your car?" he asked.

"It just died," I told him, turning the key in the ignition again. Nothing.

"Had you already pulled over when it happened?"

"No," I told him. "It died on the road, so it's probably not the battery."

"Why don't I take you into town, get you to a hotel and organize a tow?"

I quickly debated my options—spend the night with Aunt Matilda in a cramped Kia Soul, or maybe be able to take a shower and sleep in a bed. It was a short debate. "Thanks," I told him. "That would be terrific. Let me just dig out my overnight bag and we'll go." It took a little doing, but I located the red strap of my overnight bag and extracted it from the pile in the back seat, then grabbed the key from the ignition. My raincoat was buried, unfortunately, but at least I'd have a toothbrush.

"Don't you want to turn the hazard lights off?" he asked as I stood in the pouring rain. "Save your battery."

"Good idea," I said, reaching in to flick them off before following him to the cruiser.

Aunt Matilda followed, too. "This is so exciting," she burbled. "I've never been in a police cruiser before! Do you think he'll make the sirens go?"

I ignored her as best I could—the last thing I needed was to seem like I was prone to conversing with myself.

"Thanks so much for helping me out," I told the officer as I tucked my bag in under my feet. The dashboard was a mass of lights and screens; it was a little intimidating.

Aunt Matilda had passed right through the door of the car and was bouncing around in the back seat. "So this is what it feels like to be arrested!"

As my aunt poked her fingers through the metal grille separating the back from the front, I glanced over at the officer as he took the hood of his raincoat off. And... um... wow. He could have been a Hemsworth brother.

Aunt Matilda noticed, too. "He's a looker," she observed. "Maybe things are looking up for you, Amanda."

I surreptitiously wiped under my eyes in case there was any smeary mascara as he put the cruiser in drive and pulled back onto the highway. "What brings you to Misty Hollow?" he asked as he turned onto the exit.

"Strictly accidental. I'm moving to Portland, actually. Or at least I'm trying to move to Portland. They closed down 95, and then there was a detour, and the nav system got me lost, and then my car gave up the ghost."

"You do know that you're in Vermont."

I blinked. "Vermont? How did I end up in Vermont?"

"Might want to get your navigation system checked out. Good thing I happened to be driving by," he said. "I'm not usually out on the highway at night."

"Maybe your luck is turning around," Aunt Matilda suggested as she drifted through the metal grate, brushing past me on her way to investigate all the control panels. I shivered as she made contact; so did the officer, whose name I realized I didn't know.

"I'm Amanda, by the way. Amanda Blackthorne."

"Zeke Parker," he replied as we approached the small town of Misty Hollow. "There are a few Blackthornes in Misty Hollow. Sure you're not related?"

I shook my head. "Everyone in my family lives in Boston or Florida. What a cute town!" I commented as he turned onto a main street that looked like it could have been featured in a storybook. The billboard might look less than enchanting, but the town itself was gorgeous. There was a row of shops in quaint storefronts. As we rolled down the street, I noticed a bookstore with a swinging sign labeled Once Upon a Time, a bakery named Sticky Buns, with a beautiful woodland bread display in the plate window, and a corner coffee shop named Magic Beans, that had a smattering of bistro chairs and tables in front. There was also a small shop called The Crooked Broomstick, with crystals sparkling in the window; it looked like some kind of new-age store. "Is there a reasonably priced hotel?"

"There's only one hotel," he replied. "A bed and breakfast, actually. It's called Blue Water Inn. I'll drop you off and leave a message for Ed that you'll be in touch."

"Who's Ed?"

"He owns the Misty Hollow repair shop," he told me. "He'll set up a tow and get your car taken care of."

"I like this town," Aunt Matilda announced from the dashboard, where she was fiddling with the knobs. It was a good thing she was invisible to Zeke, or he wouldn't have been able to see through the windshield. "It feels nice."

It did, I realized. Something inside me had relaxed since he turned onto Main Street. It felt homey here... comfortable. As he turned onto a side street, the siren blared.

Zeke reached for the knob and flipped it off. "What the..."

Aunt Matilda was perched on the dash, with half her

body on the wrong side of the windshield, looking pleased with herself. I shot her a stern warning look. She blew me a raspberry and started to play with the video display.

Thankfully, he turned off at big, gray Victorian before Aunt Matilda managed to do any more damage. "Here we are," he said as he pulled up near the front door.

"Thank you so much," I told him as I grabbed my bag from beneath my feet.

"My pleasure," he told me. "Check with Ed at the shop tomorrow morning; I'll give the tow truck company a call, and you can square it with him. If you need anything else, here's my card."

He handed me a card, and our fingers brushed. Despite the humid air, I felt a slight shock, almost like static electricity. I thanked him, and our eyes locked for a moment. Then I grabbed my bag and, with Aunt Matilda in my wake, made a dash for the front door of the inn.

"THIS PLACE IS PRETTY NICE," Aunt Matilda commented as she swirled around the lobby. If you could call it a lobby; it looked more like a living room, complete with a banked fire in the ornate fireplace and a calico cat curled up on the Oriental rug in front of it. "Not as nice as that policeman, though. If I was twenty years younger and still alive…"

As she explored the room and commented on the visual merits of Officer Parker, I tried to decide what to do. It was two in the morning and I didn't want to wake anyone up, but I didn't want to spend the night in the lobby, either. There was no bell or button or instructions on what to do.

"Oooh, look at this sofa," Aunt Matilda said, perching on the red velvet settee. "I feel like I belong in a movie." She struck a pose, and the calico cat shot up from the rug like it had been fired from a gun. A moment later, she was atop the heavy oak hutch, staring down at Aunt Matilda with her tail puffed up like a bottle brush and hissing like a snake.

"What's up with her?" Aunt Matilda said. I didn't answer, because at that moment, a middle-aged woman walked into the lobby, eliminating my anxiety about how to let someone know I was here. She was dressed in a blue fluffy bathrobe covered in coffee cups, and looked like she'd just climbed out of bed. Which I guessed she had.

"I'm so sorry to bother you," I said, wiping my wet hair out of my eyes and trying to ignore Aunt Matilda, who was busy trying to coax the terrified cat from her perch on top of the hutch. "My car broke down on the highway, and I need a place to stay."

"That's what we're here for," the woman said in a cheery tone. "One room for the night, then?"

"Yes, please." As I spoke, the cat hissed louder. I turned to look; Aunt Matilda was floating up next to her, trying to pet her. The cat had other ideas; as I watched, she launched herself at a framed painting of a wrought-iron bench in a garden. It didn't work; the picture slewed to the side, depositing the poor cat on the floor. She scuttled under the settee, letting out a colorful melange of hisses and growls. Matilda floated down toward the floor, determined to follow her. I rolled my eyes and gave her a stern look, but it was useless.

"Please tell your friend to let Patches settle down," the woman said. "She doesn't like ghosts."

"What?" Aunt Matilda and I spoke at the same time. I swiveled to look at the innkeeper, whose eyes appeared to be on my wayward aunt. "You can see her?" I asked.

The woman nodded and looked down at her computer screen. "First floor okay?"

"That's fine," I said, as Matilda drifted up next to me.

"How can you see me?" Matilda asked. "No one's ever been able to see me before. Except Amanda."

"I just can," she said. "Always have been able to. Anyway, I'm going to put you in the Rose Room. We've got a resident spirit in the house—her name is Ivy—and she's very shy. If you stay off the second floor, we should be okay."

"There's another one of me here?" Matilda asked, brightening. You'd think ghosts were a dime a dozen, but Aunt Matilda had only turned up half a dozen of her kind over the past two years, and none of them had been what you'd call chatty.

The woman nodded. "If you're here a few days, she might be brave enough to come out, but she keeps to herself a lot."

"I'd love to meet her. How old is she?"

"She just turned 100," the woman said, as if a hundred-year-old ghost named Ivy were perfectly ordinary. "Now, here's the key. It's down that hallway to the left, and breakfast starts at eight. Do you need any help with your luggage?"

"This is all I've got," I said, pointing to my small bag.

"Great. And the Crooked Broomstick opens tomorrow at ten."

"What?"

"You'll want to visit it while you're here."

"Why? Are they hiring?" Aunt Matilda asked.

"Maybe," she said cryptically. Before I could ask her anything else, she smiled at both of us and turned off the computer. "I'm going to head back to bed. If you need anything, just dial 0 on your room phone." She smiled at both of us and turned off the computer. "I'll see you at breakfast!"

"I CAN'T BELIEVE she could see me!" Aunt Matilda said excitedly as I opened the door to the Rose Room a few minutes later. "And there's another ghost here. I can't wait to meet her!"

"Well, don't go hunting her down tonight," I admonished her as I turned on the light. The room was, predictably, a dusky rose color, with a beautiful duvet embroidered with roses and lavender. Even the air smelled faintly of roses. I dropped my bag and closed the door behind me, relieved to be in a room for the night.

"This is nice," Aunt Matilda commented as she floated around the room. She ducked into the bathroom, then flitted back out. "There's a big claw-foot tub in there; you should take a bath."

"I think I will," I said. It was late, but I was still wired from the adrenaline dump of being stranded, and my damp clothes had given me a chill.

As I walked into the spacious, tiled bathroom to turn on the tub, Aunt Matilda followed me. "I wonder what it's like where Ivy lives?"

"She told you to leave her alone," I chided Aunt Matilda as I turned on the hot water, pleased to note a bottle of bubbles. I emptied it into the tub and inhaled as the scent of roses filled the small bathroom.

"But how could she be shy around me?" she asked.

"Not everyone is quite as... effervescent as you are."

"It must be my joie de vivre," she said. "Ironic, since I'm not technically alive."

"Maybe she'll be more up for company in the morning," I suggested. "But for now, let's just settle in, okay? It's not like Ivy's going anywhere anytime soon."

As I spoke, there was a bump in the hall. A chill unrelated to my wet clothes ran down my spine.

I looked at Aunt Matilda expectantly.

"I'm not going out there," she said, eyes wide.

With a sigh, I walked over to the door and looked through the peephole. Nothing.

"Probably just pipes bumping or something," I suggested.

"That didn't sound like pipes," she said ominously.

There was another bump. I looked again.

"Open the door a crack," Aunt Matilda suggested.

"Or you could just go through the door," I reminded her.

"No way. You know how I am about ghosts and things."

"Five minutes ago you were complaining that you couldn't go meet one."

"That's a different kind of ghost."

"Fine," I said, and unlocked the deadbolt, making sure the chain was still in place.

As soon as the door opened a crack, something dark and sticky and cold flew through it. I jumped back and screamed, but it wasn't after me.

It glommed right onto Aunt Matilda's arm.

SPELL OF TROUBLE, **the first in a new paranormal cozy series, is scheduled for release Fall/Winter 2019. Check Karen's web site for updates!**

MORE BOOKS BY KAREN MACINERNEY

To download a free book and receive members-only outtakes, short stories, recipes, and updates, join Karen's Reader's Circle at www.karenmacinerney.com! You can also join her on Facebook.

And don't forget to follow her on BookBub to get newsflashes on new releases!

The Dewberry Farm Mysteries

The Gray Whale Inn Mysteries

Brush With Death
Death Runs Adrift
Whale of a Crime
Claws for Alarm
Scone Cold Dead
Cookbook: The Gray Whale Inn Kitchen
Blueberry Blues (A Gray Whale Inn Short Story)
Pumpkin Pied (A Gray Whale Inn Short Story)
Iced Inn (A Gray Whale Inn Short Story)

The Margie Peterson Mysteries

Mother's Day Out
Mother Knows Best
Mother's Little Helper

Tales of an Urban Werewolf

Howling at the Moon
On the Prowl
Leader of the Pack

Six Merry Little Murders: A Cozy Christmas Bundle
(October 2019)

And coming Fall/Winter 2019... a new paranormal cozy series
featuring Amanda Blackthorne and her spectral Aunt Matilda!

RECIPES

APPLE PUFF PANCAKE WITH CINNAMON BUTTER MAPLE SYRUP

Ingredients:

Apple Puff Pancake

1 apple, thinly sliced
1 tablespoon brown sugar
6 tablespoons unsalted butter, melted
4 eggs
2/3 cups whole milk
2/3 cup all-purpose flour
2 teaspoons vanilla extract
3/4 teaspoon cinnamon
1/2 teaspoon kosher salt
whipped cream, for serving

Cinnamon Butter Maple Syrup
1/2 cup maple syrup
2 tablespoons unsalted butter
1/2 teaspoon cinnamon
1/2 teaspoon vanilla extract

Directions:

Puff Pancake

Preheat the oven to 450 degrees F. Arrange the apple slices in the bottom a 10-12 inch oven-proof skillet. Drizzle 4 table-spoons of melted butter over the apples and sprinkle with brown sugar. Place the skillet on the center rack of the oven for 10 minutes.

While skillet is in the oven, in a blender, combine the eggs, milk, flour, vanilla, cinnamon, salt and the remaining 2 tablespoons melted butter. Blend on high for 30 seconds to one minute or until the batter is smooth, with no large clumps of flour. Remove the hot skillet from the oven and pour the batter into the skillet, then place the skillet on a lower rack of the oven and bake for 18-20 minutes or until the pancake is fully puffed and browned on top. (Do not open the oven during the first 15 minutes of cooking or the pancake may deflate.) Remove the puff pancake from the oven and serve topped with cinnamon syrup.

Cinnamon Butter Maple Syrup

In a small saucepan, combine the maple, butter, and cinnamon and bring to a boil over high heat. Reduce the heat to medium and simmer for 3-5 minutes. Remove from the heat and stir in the vanilla. Serve warm aside the puff pancake.

CRANBERRY ISLAND CRABMEAT QUICHE

Ingredients:

1 deep unbaked pastry shell (9 inches) or buttery quiche crust, below
1 cup shredded Swiss cheese, divided
1/2 cup chopped sweet red pepper
1/4 cup chopped green onions
1 tablespoon butter
3 large eggs
1-1/2 cups half-and-half cream
1/2 teaspoon salt
1/4 teaspoon pepper
1/2 teaspoon Old Bay seasoning
3/4 cup crabmeat, chopped

Directions:

Preheat oven 450°. Line a pastry shell with a double thickness of heavy-duty foil and bake for 5 minutes. Remove foil and bake 5 minutes longer, then immediately sprinkle 1/2 cup cheese over crust. Reduce oven heat to 375°. In a skillet, saute red pepper and onions in butter on medium-high heat until tender. While veggies are cooking, in a large bowl, whisk the eggs, cream, salt, pepper, and Old Bay seasoning. Stir in the crab, red pepper mixture and remaining cheese, and pour into crust.

Bake for 30-35 minutes or until a knife inserted in the center comes out clean. Let stand for 15 minutes before cutting.

Buttery Pastry Shell

1 1/4 cups all-purpose flour
1/4 teaspoon salt
1/2 cup butter, chilled and diced
1/4 cup ice water

Directions:

In a large bowl, combine flour and salt, then cut in butter until mixture resembles coarse crumbs. Stir in water, a tablespoon at a time, until mixture forms a ball. Wrap in plastic and refrigerate for 4 hours or overnight.

When dough is chilled, roll out to fit a 9 inch pie plate. Place crust in pie plate. Press the dough evenly into the bottom and sides of the pie plate.

CHOCOLATE CHERRY HAZELNUT SCONES

Ingredients:

2 cups all-purpose flour
1/3 cup packed brown sugar
1 1/2 teaspoons baking powder
1/2 teaspoon baking soda
1/4 teaspoon salt
6 tablespoons unsalted butter, chilled
1/2 cup buttermilk
1 egg
1 teaspoon vanilla extract (preferably Mexican vanilla)
1 teaspoon almond extract
1/2 cup semisweet chocolate chips
1/2 cup milk chocolate chips
1/2 cup chopped toasted hazelnuts
1/4 cup dried sweet cherries
Turbinado sugar for sprinkling

Directions:

Preheat oven to 400 degrees and lightly butter a 9-inch diameter circle in the center of a baking sheet. In a large bowl, stir together flour, brown sugar, baking powder, baking soda, and salt. Cut the butter into 1/2-inch cubes, and distribute evenly over flour mixture. With a pastry blender or two knives, cut butter into the flour mixture. Stir together buttermilk, egg, and extract; add to the flour mixture, and stir to combine. Stir in the chocolate chips and hazelnuts (the dough will be sticky).

Spread the dough into an 8 inch diameter circle (inside the buttered circle) on the baking sheet and cut into 8 wedges with a serrated knife. Sprinkle with Turbinado sugar, then bake scones for 17 to 19 minutes, or until the top is lightly browned. Cool on baking sheet for 5 minutes, then transfer scones to the wire rack to cool and cut into wedges. Best served warm!

LEMON BLUEBERRY SUNBURST SCONES

Ingredients:

Scones

2 cups all-purpose flour, plus more for hands and work surface
1/2 cup granulated sugar
1 Tablespoon fresh lemon zest (about 1 lemon)
2 and 1/2 teaspoons baking powder
1/2 teaspoon salt
1/2 cup unsalted butter, frozen
1/2 cup heavy cream (plus 2 Tbsp for brushing)
1 large egg
1 and 1/2 teaspoons pure vanilla extract
1 heaping cup fresh or frozen blueberries (do not thaw)
Coarse sugar (for sprinkling)

Lemon Icing

1 cup confectioners' sugar

3 Tablespoons fresh lemon juice

Directions:

Scones

Whisk flour, sugar, lemon zest, baking powder, and salt together in a large bowl. Grate the frozen butter using a box grater, then add it to the flour mixture and combine with a pastry cutter, two forks, or your fingers, until the mixture comes together in pea-sized crumbs. Put dough in the refrigerator or freezer as you mix the wet ingredients together.

Whisk 1/2 cup heavy cream, egg, and vanilla extract in a small bowl. Drizzle over the flour mixture, add the blueberries, then mix together until everything appears just moistened.

Pour dough onto the counter and, with floured hands, work it into a ball. The dough will be sticky; if it's too sticky, add a little more flour. If it seems too dry, add 1-2 more tablespoons of heavy cream. Press finished dough into an 8-inch disc and cut into 8 wedges.

Brush scones with remaining heavy cream and sprinkle with coarse sugar. Preheat oven to 400°F and place scones on a plate or lined baking sheet and refrigerate for at least 15 minutes. (If you want fresh scones in the morning, you can refrigerate them overnight.) Line a large baking sheet with parchment paper or a silicone baking mat. After refrigerating, arrange scones 2-3 inches apart on the prepared baking sheet(s) and bake for 22-25 minutes or until golden brown around the edges and lightly browned on top. Remove scones from the oven and cool for a few minutes before topping with lemon icing.

Icing

Whisk the icing ingredients together. Drizzle over warm scones.

BONUS RECIPE: MAPLE WALNUT SCONES

Ingredients:

3 cups all purpose flour
4 tablespoons dark brown sugar
1 1/2 teaspoons baking powder
1/2 teaspoon baking soda
1/2 teaspoon salt
3/4 cup chilled unsalted butter, cut into 1/2-inch pieces
1/2 cup plus 6 tablespoons whipping cream, more as needed
1/2 cup plus 2 tablespoons pure maple syrup
2/3 cup powdered sugar
1/2 cup walnuts

Directions:

Preheat oven to 375°F. Whisk flour, 2 tablespoons dark brown sugar, baking powder, baking soda and salt in large bowl to blend. Add butter and rub in with fingertips until mixture resembles coarse meal. Stir 1/2 cup whipping cream and 1/2 cup maple syrup in small bowl to blend.

Gradually add cream mixture to flour mixture, stirring just until dough comes together and adding more cream by tablespoonfuls if dough is dry. Turn dough out onto lightly floured surface. Knead dough gently until smooth, about 5 turns. Using floured hands, pat out dough to form an 8-inch round; cut dough into 8 wedges. Transfer wedges to baking sheet, spacing 2 inches apart.

Bake scones for about 20 minutes, until golden and toothpick inserted into center comes out clean. Transfer to rack.

Meanwhile, whisk remaining 2 tablespoons dark brown sugar, 6 tablespoons whipping cream and 2 tablespoons maple syrup in medium bowl to blend. Gradually whisk in enough powdered sugar to form thick glaze.

Drizzle or spread glaze over warm scones. Let stand until glaze sets.

ACKNOWLEDGMENTS

First, many thanks to my family, not just for putting up with me, but for continuing to come up with creative ways to kill people. (You should see the looks we get in restaurants.) And thank you to Andy Krell for coming up with the idea of centering a story around a fisheries observer!

Special thanks to the MacInerney Mystery Mavens (who help with all manner of things, from covers to concepts), particularly Alicia Farage, Carol Swartz, Mandy Young Kutz, Kay Pucciarelli, Marissa Lee, Samantha Mann, Pat Warren Tewalt, Barbara Tobey, and Azanna Wishart, for their careful reading of the manuscript. What would I do without you???

Thanks (as always) to Bob Dombrowski for his incredible artwork. Kim Killion, as always, did an amazing job putting together the cover design, and Randy Ladenheim-Gil's sharp editorial eye helped keep me from embarrassing myself. And finally, thank you to ALL of the wonderful readers who make Gray Whale Inn possible, especially my fabulous Facebook community. You keep me going!

ABOUT THE AUTHOR

Karen is the housework-impaired, award-winning author of multiple mystery series, and her victims number well into the double digits. She lives in Austin, Texas with her sassy family, Tristan, and Little Bit (a.k.a. Dog #1 and Dog #2).

Feel free to visit Karen's web site at www. karenmacinerney.com, where you can download a free book and sign up for her Readers' Circle to receive subscriber-only short stories, deleted scenes, recipes and other bonus material. You can also find her on Facebook (she spends an inordinate amount of time there), where Karen loves getting to know her readers, answering questions, and offering quirky, behind-the-scenes looks at the writing process (and life in general).

P. S. Don't forget to follow Karen on BookBub to get newsflashes on new releases!

www.karenmacinerney.com
karen@karenmacinerney.com

facebook.com/AuthorKarenMacInerney

twitter.com/KarenMacInerney

Made in the USA
Middletown, DE
07 March 2020

85972335R00146